IF YOU'VE EVER WORKED IN AN OFFICE, YOU'LL RECOGNIZE THESE LADIES

Jane Fonda

JUDY BERNLY—Newly divorced and taking the first job of her life. After a couple of sessions at the copying machine, she's ready for tranquilizers.

Lily Tomlin

VIOLET NEWSTEAD—Her boss is stealing her ideas while ordering her to get his coffee. After 12 years of getting nowhere, she's ready to stir things up.

Dolly Parton

DORALEE RHODES—Executive secretary, dedicated to her job. When she learns the stories the boss is telling about her, she's ready to blow the whistle.

Twentieth Century-Fox presents

AN IPC FILMS PRODUCTION OF A
COLIN HIGGINS PICTURE

JANE   LILY   DOLLY
FONDA   TOMLIN   PARTON

in

NINE TO FIVE

DABNEY COLEMAN
ELIZABETH WILSON
and
STERLING HAYDEN
as
Chairman of the Board

Produced by
BRUCE GILBERT

Directed by
COLIN HIGGINS

Screenplay by
COLIN HIGGINS and PATRICIA RESNICK

Story by
PATRICIA RESNICK

Music by
CHARLES FOX

NINE
TO
FIVE

THOM RACINA

Based on the Screenplay by
COLIN HIGGINS and PATRICIA RESNICK

From a Story by
PATRICIA RESNICK

BANTAM BOOKS
TORONTO · NEW YORK · LONDON

NINE TO FIVE
A Bantam Book / December 1980

ISBN 0–553–14496–0

Published simultaneously in the United States and Canada

*Bantam Books are published by Bantam Books, Inc. Its trade-
mark, consisting of the words "Bantam Books" and the por-
trayal of a bantam, is Registered in U.S. Patent and Trademark
Office and in other countries. Marca Registrada. Bantam
Books, Inc., 666 Fifth Avenue, New York, New York 10103.*

PRINTED IN THE UNITED STATES OF AMERICA

0 9 8 7 6 5 4 3 2 1

for "Penelope" and "Henrietta"—
Pat Rupp and Pat Calvert—
my favorite secretaries

NINE
TO
FIVE

Prologue

Judy Radman was right on schedule.

"General Hospital" had just broken for its third commercial, and Judy was within three squirts of icing the chocolate cake she'd promised Dick for dinner.

Judy had it all figured out. She emptied the dishwasher of last night's dishes, put them away, loaded the breakfast cups and plates and planned the day's menu during "All My Children." "One Life To Live" meant doing the laundry, ironing, and applying a daily facial. The baking—conjuring up exotic desserts for her sweet-toothed husband—was always finished early, during "Search For Tomorrow."

But "General Hospital" was prime time for Judy. She never scheduled any chore that might distract her while the show was on. Sometimes, like today, she'd allow herself something simple to do, like icing the cake. Her eyes were riveted to the tube, hoping that Monica would finally reveal the truth to Rick in today's episode. If Monica didn't, Judy wouldn't be able to stand the suspense until Monday.

And then it happened. Monica knocked once, opened the door, and faced Rick with tears in her eyes. Judy's interest was so intense, she didn't even hear Dick's car pull into the driveway. She was so completely involved with Monica, she never heard Dick cut the motor, slam the car door, and shuffle across the living room into the kitchen.

The highlight of Dick's life had been that moment

—years ago—when he'd scored the winning touchdown for Ohio State against Michigan. But the ex-football star had sat on the bench ever since he graduated from school, and looked it. His features were still All-American, but his slightly sagging jowls and more-than-slightly sagging beltline were evidence of the cosmetic effects of seven-layer cakes and six packs.

As Dick slumped into the breakfast nook, Judy, eyes still glued to the tube, raised a hand to silence Dick's as yet unspoken greeting.

Dick bit his lower lip for a second, then leaned forward and tapped Judy on the shoulder. "Judy, I've got to talk to you," he said in a strained tone.

"Shh!" Judy muttered, then blinked at the screen. *"Oh, my God, Monica!"*

"Damn it, Judy." Dick grabbed her by the shoulders.

"Monica, you can't!"

Dick reached over and clicked off the TV.

"Dick!" She looked at him for the first time. She was back to reality. What was he doing home at this hour?

"I said I've *got* to talk to you."

She wanted to turn the set back on. "But there's only a few minutes left and I'll just *die* if Monica doesn't—"

"Judy, this is *serious*."

Judy stared at him, then drew a deep breath. "You lost your job."

He nodded. "The business is going under. We've all been laid off. I'm broke."

She remembered the very same thing happening last week on "All My Children." "Dick, you can always—"

"No, don't say anything. There's more."

Judy swallowed hard. The car was being repossessed. Yes, that had to be it. No, the mortgage. He hadn't been paying the mortgage. They were foreclosing on the house. If only she'd listened to her mother always telling her *she* should handle the accounts. Well, she could take it. And she would help him be strong. "Dick, you can tell me. I'll understand."

He looked into her eyes and half whispered. "This isn't easy."

"Of course it isn't. We'll work it out."

"There's nothing to work out. I want a divorce."

Judy opened her mouth to say something, but no words came. She heard only the sound of the pastry bag burping in her tightly clenched fists as a mountain of creamy frosting oozed over Dick's sport jacket.

The Norma Lane Employment Agency was crowded even after office hours. During the day it was a mob scene, a mélange of job seekers, some headed for interviews, most waiting hopelessly for a call. Judy was taking a typing test, as nervous as the day the judge had told her that her marriage was dissolved.

A big black woman dressed all in white came up and pulled the sheet of paper right out of Judy's typewriter. "Sorry, honey, time's up. I'll grade this. You can take a seat till a counselor calls you."

Judy was feeling more than a little intimidated when an overweight blonde lady with the thickest glasses Judy had ever seen came around the corner and read from a chart. "Judy Bernly?"

"Yes."

"Over here."

Judy walked up to her. The woman smiled. "Come over to my desk."

"Yes, ma'am." Judy nervously sat on the edge of the wooden chair facing the desk.

"I see you wrote *Radman* and crossed it out. You divorced?"

"Yes. Just recently. I'm still unsure of what to put down."

"I know the feeling. Divorced twice myself." She reached out a hand. "Name's Clara Cross. Men are a pain, believe me, I know. What you gotta do now is go on, and single is the only way to do it." She went back to the chart. "Now, let's see . . . address. You own the apartment?"

"No. Rent. I just moved in."

"Kids?"

"No."

"Alimony?"

"No."

Clara looked up with a frown.

"You see, my husband was in partnership with—"

The phone rang and cut Judy off as Clara answered it. "Just a sec, honey—hello. Yes, Joanie. All right, hold the line, I'll transfer you to Susan." Clara held the receiver to her breast and shouted to another desk. "Susan! TCC on four. Old man Powers is looking for a new secretary. Same type: tits and ass and early twenties."

Judy squirmed and pushed her glasses up on her nose.

Susan yelled back, "Body by Fisher and brain by Tinkertoy. I got it." She picked up the phone.

Clara hung up. "They're always looking for the young ones," she said to Judy. "Now, where were we?" She checked the chart again. "Three years of college. That's good. What was your major?"

"American history."

"That's *not* so good. Previous experience ... summer camp counselor?"

"I taught tennis."

"That all?"

"A little swimming."

"No, I mean have you had any other work experience?"

Apologetically, Judy said, "No. Just a housewife. I got married right out of college."

The black woman brought over the corrected typing tests. "Here's the scores, Clara."

Clara looked them over without giving a hint to Judy as to how they turned out. Then she said, "Tell me what kind of work you're looking for."

"Well, I thought a nice little job, administrative assistant, maybe executive secretary. Something that pays around twenty thousand a year."

Clara coughed. "Hey, whoa, slow down. Let me set you straight. Your test scores aren't bad, but not

that terrific. You've no previous experience, no special
skills, age-wise in the job market you're over the hill,
and you're a woman. You're not worth twenty thou
out there, honey. You'll be lucky if you get nine or
ten."

"Oh my God. I don't think I can live on that."

Clara flipped through the file behind her desk.
"Okay, let's see what I can do for you. Here's one. No,
this won't work, bookkeeping and typing at the Oaks
Cleaners. They always end up getting the girl to press
pants and blouses when the clerical work runs out.
How about ... well, you tell me. How about doing
some office work for a painters' supply house? I gotta
warn ya, though, those guys are animals. No girl has
lasted in that job over three weeks."

"I don't think it's for me."

Clara continued to dig. "Well, we'll find something. ABC Carriers—no, the boss is a madman.
Main office of Bettleson Bakeries—what is this doing
in here? They went out of business three months ago.
Let's see ... hmm, B&W Industries—your scores aren't
high enough for them. Cabaret Video Concepts—your
scores aren't *low* enough for them. Actually, we send
them girls who can't type at all. You know the kind,
can't remember their own names, but have the right
stats—38–24–38? And the head of the company always calls back to tell me how 'perfectly' she's working out."

Judy squirmed.

"We call those gals the 'Liz Ray Typing Pool.'
Ah, here's something—clerical worker at Consolidated. A big company. Light typing, filing, free parking,
medical plan, profit sharing." Clara looked to Judy,
who smiled enthusiastically. "Seven-fifty a month. Not
bad to start. What do you say?"

Judy looked stricken, but tried to sound encour-
aged. "Well, I didn't know the pay would be so low."

Clara pulled the card from the file and leaned
over the desk. Judy leaned forward. "Listen, take my
advice," Clara said, girl-to-girl. "I see many women in
your position, more every day. You're on your own.

You need a job. Now it's your choice, you either look at it as a burden or as a great new adventure. You choose."

Judy sat up straight. Her voice was a little hesitating. "A clerical worker?"

Clara leaned back. "You in or out, honey?"

Judy thought for a moment, then announced, "I'm in."

"Great!" Clara extended her hand. "Welcome to the world of nine to five."

One

Judy moved through the glut of people in the lobby, pushing her way to the elevators marked *Floors 12–37*. When the doors opened, she found herself swept to the rear of the elevator, hoping someone would push the button marked *15* so she wouldn't have to reach over the sea of shoulders to get to it. Her prayer was answered. A short, young woman who looked half-asleep, touched *15* and the doors closed.

Judy listened to the conversations on the way up.

"Well, another day." And a moan.

"I start vacation next week, thank the Lord."

"If they haven't repaired the machine yet, I'm simply refusing to cart those files down to twelve and feed them to *that* machine one-by-one."

"Damn right."

" . . . and didja see the picture of Hinkle and his wife in the paper this morning? Some charity ball or something. Donating the money he doesn't pay us."

"I'm *so* zonked out today, Harriet. Kip and I got into a really heavy discussion of the martial arts last night and before we knew it, the sun was coming up."

"I wanna *throw* up. Just the thought of another day in this place makes me sick."

The doors opened on fifteen.

"Excuse me, please." Judy squeezed her way through, just making it out before the doors closed. Alone in the corridor, she straightened her little hat

and took a deep breath. Then she pulled the paper
from her purse again and read the name on it. She
turned left and headed toward the Personnel Office.

Inside that very office, Violet Newstead was
scowling at the file the personnel director had just
handed her. "But Norman," she moaned, "she's never
worked a day in her life before." Her voice was soft
yet the effect was striking. Tall, with sparkling eyes
and high cheekbones, she was a lovely looking woman
whose personality shined. With dark auburn hair,
efficiently styled, well-tailored but fashionable clothes,
she was the embodiment of a tactful and diplomatic
businesswoman. But she had a way of making people
laugh—with witty asides, double entendres, remarks
that sailed right over heads—that gained the love of
nearly everyone in the office. But today she wasn't
feeling particularly humorous. "Come on, Norman, hiring someone who hasn't worked one crummy day,
that's not fair."

"I thought you'd be more sympathetic."

"I am sympathetic. But why do *I* have to train
her? Let her work in someone else's section. I don't
have the time to do it myself."

"Her typing's okay," Norman pointed out. "And
she has three years of college behind her—"

"American history major, big deal! When we're in
a bind upstairs, I'll have her recite the Gettysburg
Address."

"Okay, okay." Norman's tone was placating.
Through the glass partition separating the inner and
outer offices, Norman watched as Judy entered and
talked to the receptionist. "She's here now. Let's see
how she stacks up."

"Hmm," Violet deadpanned. "Interesting choice
of words. Is that why you hired her?"

Norman laughed.

Violet stood up and looked through the glass.
Judy seemed younger than the early thirties her appli-
cation noted her to be. Girlish and thin, she had the
legginess of a newborn fawn, and some of the awkward-

ness as well. Her huge blue eyes overcame a pretty but nervous smile.

Norman stood up and gazed out at her.

"She's a looker alright. Yeah. Looks like Donna Reed."

Violet noticed Judy was dressed about a decade out of synch, strangely old-fashioned for a woman so young and attractive. She had on a blue and pink flowered suit with—God forbid—a pink carnation in the lapel. There was a big bow tied around the collar, and her curly ash-blonde hair was overcome by a clumsy hat. And she had a seed pearl chain attached to her eyeglasses. "Give me the strength," Violet moaned. She moved to the outer office and forced a smile, though she remained cool and businesslike. "Judy Bernly?"

Judy peered through her glasses at Violet's long, slim, efficient-looking figure. "Yes."

"I'm Violet. Violet Newstead. I'll be showing you around and training you. Welcome to Consolidated." She glanced back at Norman. "I'm sure you'll *love* it here."

"Thank you," Judy said, warmly.

"Well, come on, I'll give you the tour." They left the office and walked down the corridor.

"This is quite a day for me," Judy said. "I was so nervous, I left an hour earlier to be here on time."

"How nice."

"I'm glad I did, because it took me forty-five minutes to find a parking place."

"We park here in the building, so you won't have that hassle from now on. Here, I'll show you how to punch in." They turned into an alcove which was lined with metal slots which held time cards. Violet opened a cabinet and pulled out a fresh one, wrote Judy's name at the top with the pencil she kept stuck in her hair, and inserted it into the machine. "A clock that bites," she muttered as the machine clicked and spit the card back into her hand.

She placed it into a slot under a sign that said

CLERICAL—FLOOR 16. "That's all there is to it, when you come in, when you go to lunch, when you get back, and when you leave at five. Breaks don't need to be punched, because there's always a watchdog named Rosalind who considers it her duty to report anyone lolling over coffee for more than fifteen minutes."

"I understand."

"I don't." Violet motioned for Judy to follow her toward the elevators. "So where do you live?"

"I just moved into an apartment near the airport."

"Some nice places out there, I hear."

"They're not as expensive as in the city."

"Yeah, but who wants a DC-10 landing on your roof?"

Judy was about to reply, but a young, black mail clerk came by, pushing a delivery basket filled with manila envelopes. "Hey, there, Violet, what's shakin'? What do ya hear about your promotion?"

"Nothing yet. Eddie Smith, Judy Bernly. Judy starts work today."

"Hello," Judy said.

Eddie shook his head and kicked the basket. "Oh, man! How am I ever gonna bust outta that mail room prison if they keep hiring people from the outside?" He looked Judy in the eye. "You're gonna hate it here." And he pushed the cart off as the elevator doors opened.

Violet and Judy stepped inside. The doors closed. Violet punched *16*. "We're on the next floor up. Then above us is the Executive Suite, where the President, Mr. Hinkle, is, and the Chairman of the Board." She ran her fingers through her reddish-brown hair.

"It all sounds so . . . big."

"Yes, I suppose it is. I've been here twelve years and I've never *seen* the Chairman of the Board."

"Twelve years!" Judy had a premonition of never seeing the soap operas again for twelve whole years. "Can I ask you about salary? I don't think I can live on—"

Violet cut her off. "That's a touchy subject around here. You'll have to take it up with our boss, Mr. Hart."

"Oh. Sorry."

The elevator stopped. Violet gave her a wink. "Don't worry. You'll get the hang of it."

Judy smiled.

Violet didn't. "*Then* you'll be sorry." Violet stepped out and watched Judy enter the main office.

It was like a football field with a roof of fluorescent light suspended over it, the long rows of desks stretching in a grid square pattern to the far walls. On the sides were glass-paneled offices with private secretary desks in front of them, separated by low dividers. Typewriters—hundreds of them—and key punches typed out a fast rhythm to which the whole floor moved like an anthill of activity.

Violet gestured for Judy to follow her into the labyrinth, but before they took a step, a tweedy, long-legged woman with her hair in a bun called out, "*Oh, Violet!*" Her voice reminded Judy of somebody scratching their fingernails on a blackboard. "*Violet, just a minute!*"

The woman came up to them. "I've been meaning to talk to you about Mr. Hart's rules on office decor. We seem to be getting a bit lax in your section."

Violet crossed her arms. "Really, Roz? How do you mean?"

"Well, I've typed it up here . . . ." Roz pulled a long sheet of typewritten rules seemingly out of nowhere. And she started to read them in her grating tone. " 'No coffee cups on the desks, no personal items left in view, no photos, plants, et cetera.' "

Violet shot Judy a look.

Roz droned on. "We mustn't look cluttered or sloppy. An office that looks efficient *is* efficient, as Mr. Hart is fond of saying." Suddenly, Roz noticed Judy. "Oh, hello."

Violet unfolded her arms. "Judy, this is Roz—Rosalind—Keith, Mr. Hart's administrative assistant. I mentioned her name before."

"Yes, I remember," Judy said, extending a hand to Roz.

Violet added, "Judy is starting today."

"Hello," Judy said, "nice to meet you."

"Consolidated welcomes you!" Roz barked.

"Our cheerleader," Violet quipped.

With just a touch too much enthusiasm, Roz added, "I hope you enjoy it here. We're all a pretty happy bunch."

"Thanks," Judy replied.

Violet rubbed her nose. "We're a bunch all right."

"Here, Violet," Roz said, handing her the type-written sheet of rules, "you can put this up on the bulletin board."

"Thanks, Roz," Violet muttered. "I know just where to *stick it*."

Roz cocked her head toward Judy. "And, Judy, if there is *anything* I can do to help you settle in, just drop on by." And with that, she hurried away.

Violet touched Judy's shoulder in warning. "One thing you should know about dear old Roz is she's the eyes, ears, nose, and throat of Mr. Hart. Anything she hears, he hears."

"You mean she's the company spy?"

"All I'm saying is if you ever want to gossip in the ladies' room, you'd better first check under the stalls for her shoes. You can't miss her lace-up ox-fords."

Judy smiled doubtfully. "Oh."

"Come on, let's cut through the battlefield." Violet headed down the main aisle of the huge room. "The section is broken down into three zones, each with a supervisor. As senior, the other two supervisors report to me and I report to Mr. Hart." She pointed to the right side of the room. "His office is over there. He's just been made a vice president. Never seen anyone leap-frog so fast to the top. I remember when he was just a management trainee." Then she let her voice drop an octave. "In fact, I trained him."

Judy looked around. A woman smiled at her and she nodded back. It was the sleepy girl from the elevator. She saw a few men at desks, young male secretaries she hadn't noticed when she first came in. She saw more hands moving on more keyboards than she ever had imagined she'd see in her life.

Violet guided Judy to her zone. Seven people worked in the area, none showing much interest in meeting a new co-worker. "Here," Violet said, "I want you to meet Betty Stokes."

Betty Stokes, a pleasant-looking black girl, nodded. "Honey, think I can talk ya into taking the kitchen detail over for me?"

"This is Judy Bernly," Violet said, "and she's got filing to learn, Betty. And this is Margaret Foster."

Margaret Foster seemed to slump in her chair. She was pecking away at her typewriter to the tune of approximately two words per minute. She looked up, brought a hand to her forehead and rubbed hard, then gave Judy something which looked like a nod.

"What's wrong with her?" Judy whispered.

"Pain."

"Headaches?"

"Jack Daniels."

A woman looked up from the adjacent desk. "I'm Maria Delgrado."

"Judy Bernly. How do you do?"

"I would tell you the truth, but Violet's my boss and I can't say those things in front of her."

Violet laughed. "The empty desk here next to Maria is where you'll sit. And this is Tom Wood."

Tom had a pencil between his teeth. " 'ello."

"Hi," Judy said.

"And Barbara Adams," Violet continued.

"Honey," Barbara said with a huge smile, "you take it easy now, hear? Violet knows, you can get real frazzled your first few weeks. You have any problems, you just come to me. I'll fix ya up."

"Thank you." Judy turned to Violet. "She seems so warm and friendly."

"Yeah. And she's the floor's Valium connection. And this is Lee Chang and Charlotte Witherspoon."

Neither one acknowledged Judy's presence. Their

noses were buried in work they didn't seem to enjoy, judging from the expressions on their faces.

"Everyone seems so . . . occupied," Judy commented.

"Yeah, well, Roz is on my case, and they all know it. We're overworked right now—Hart likes to keep it that way. If you learn fast, you'll be a big help to the whole section."

"I'll try my best."

Violet took a deep breath. "Well, I suppose you should meet Mr. Hart."

"What's he like?"

"You'll see."

Judy saw.

Even to an impartial observer, Franklin Hart appeared to be bad news. From his sweaty forehead to his elevator shoes, he was a man who reeked of smarmy distrust.

Violet introduced Judy. Hart shook her hand with his wet palm, patted her on the back as though she were one of the "gang," and grinned so every tooth in his mouth was visible. "Why don't you two gals have a seat over there." He pointed to the vinyl-covered sofa under the stag head mounted on the wood-paneled wall. He went behind hs desk and lit a cigar.

Violet whispered, "He's gonna pontificate now."

She was right. "I suppose, Judy," Hart pontificated, "that if there is a word that describes my philosophy of business, it's *teamwork*." He drew deeply on his cigar. "Isn't that right, Violet?"

"That's *one* word for it, Mr. Hart," Violet replied sweetly.

"Everyone pulling together, hey, Judy? I like to think of myself as the skipper around here, running a tight ship, but a happy one. A little Captain Bligh when necessary. When not, a little Captain Kangaroo. Ha ha ha."

Violet whispered. "We're supposed to laugh."

Judy laughed heartily.

"Now, seriously," Hart added, "and I've always

said this, it's a shame you girls didn't play football. I remember Coach Frye used to say, 'A chain is only as good as its weakest link.' And I've always—" He cut himself short. He got up and his chair wobbled. "Hmm. There's something wrong with this chair." He turned to them again. "Listen, I don't want to bore you with a long harangue. Suffice it to say it is a *jungle* out there, but if we all work together as a team, we can cut the balls off the competition—"

Judy's eyes blinked wide.

"—and be sitting pretty on top of the hill." He walked over to Judy and shook her hand again.

She felt her palm getting wet. "Thank you, I'm happy to be here."

"You're a welcome addition," he bellowed, "and an exceptionally pretty one, if I may say so."

Judy felt flattered, smarmy hand or not. "Thank you so much."

"No, I mean that," Hart said. "You should see some of the crones that have come through here lately, right, Violet?"

Violet shot him a look.

"Oh, by the way, Violet. My wife's coming by today and I want to get a nice little present for her. Could you pick her up a nice scarf or something?" He reached into his pocket and pulled out a wad of bills clipped with a gold "H."

"Mr. Hart, we've been through this before. I don't think it is my place—"

"Violet, goddammit! I've spent five minutes talking about teamwork and right away you're not there for the handoff."

Violet stood up and put her hands on her hips. "All I'm saying, Mr. Hart, is my job description doesn't say anything about making purchases for your wife."

"And all I'm saying, Violet, is that I want people around me who can cooperate and get along." He yanked his cigar out of his mouth and waved it at her. "So when I ask an employee to help me out, particularly an employee who wants to be promoted to management, I except a little cooperation. Savvy?"

"I savvy," she mumbled. She took the money.

"Good girl," Hart beamed. "We're talking silk something. Blue—maybe red—stripes."

"I think I know what you want."

"Thanks, Violet. You're the best." He turned to Judy. "You know, she was the first person I met at the company. Knows more about how it operates than Mr. Hinkle himself." He flicked his ash into the ash tray on the desk. "Well, Judy, feel free to drop in anytime you have something on your mind. That's why I have my office on this floor. I like to be close to 'my girls.' "

"There's a couple of *guys* out there too, you know," Violet snapped.

"Figure a speech, Vi, figure a speech."

Violet cringed. Without another word, she opened the door and ushered Judy out. But before she closed it, Hart yelled, "Is Doralee back yet?"

"No." Violet pursed her lips. She knew what was coming.

"Well then, bring me a cup of coffee, Violet, no sugar. Just that Skinny & Sweet."

Violet closed the door and looked at Judy. "Well, that's Franklin Hart, Junior. But to me he'll always be *F. Hart*. Period."

While Judy let Violet's remark sink in, a young woman wearing a tight pink knitted dress, so snug it looked like fuzzy skin, approached them. "Hi, Violet," she said in a little-girl voice. "How's it going?"

"Hello, Doralee. Your boss wants coffee." Violet's voice was gravelly.

"Okay," Doralee said pleasantly, putting her purse down behind her desk.

As Doralee bent over, Judy lifted her glasses to her nose. She couldn't believe the size of the woman's bosom. Doralee was sexy, and she dressed to complement her natural endowments. She had a wide smile as well, with a warm nature and naturally effervescent personality. "I just came back from gassing up his car," Doralee explained. "If I'm not filling one tank, I'm filling the other."

Judy smirked.

"This is Judy Bernly," Violet said. "She'll be working over in my section. Doralee Rhodes."

Doralee was warm in her greeting. "Well, hi, Judy. I hope everyone's been treating you real friendly and showing you around." She had a strong country accent, which was rather unexpected, because her teased, frothy blonde hair and full makeup weren't exactly down home. Around her neck she wore a gold chain with her name written in script.

"Yes," Judy responded, "everyone's been very nice." Judy couldn't seem to take her eyes off the woman's enormous bust.

"Great. If there's anything I can do, you just give a holler. I know what it's like to be the new girl in town." Doralee flashed a big smile, and headed to the coffee maker in the kitchen.

"Well," Judy said, "if all the people are as nice as you and Doralee, I'm going to be very happy here." Then she looked down to her own modest attributes and shrugged.

"Happiness is a four letter word around here," Violet replied. "Come on, let's put you to work."

Two

It wasn't easy.

Judy's typewriter jammed four times in the first hour. Somehow her little finger kept striking the *TAB* and *Q* at the same time.

She spun her Rolodex so hard all the cards flipped out into her face.

Both times she answered the phone, she forgot to push the "hold" button before transferring the call, and disconnected the line.

She had a terrible time with a report that included several lists of numbers and was whiting-out a mistake just as a bell rang. It startled her and she poured the contents of the bottle of Liquid Paper into the typewriter.

Margaret, who was getting up from her desk for lunch, called over to her. "Take it from a pro, honey. Go to the ladies' john and get yourself a Kotex and just let it soak up in there while you grab a bite to eat."

Judy looked startled.

"No big deal," Margaret said, "it'll work like new."

And it did. Judy was sopping up the white liquid under the platen when Violet walked up. "Judy, time to eat. What are you doing?"

"Nothing." She smiled and dropped her glasses to hang from the chain. "I'm coming." She picked up her purse. "I didn't know we all ate at one time."

"A floor at a time. Like being in kindergarten.

Come with me, we'll eat together. Did you bring something?"

"No."

"That's okay. They've got all kinds of things in the machines in the lunch room, but the prices, ugh. Most of the kids bring theirs."

"Thanks for the tip."

They walked down the aisle, toward the elevators. "Judy, there's one thing I should tell you."

"What's that?"

"The machine you're using. It's a Selectric II. It corrects itself automatically. You don't need liquid."

Judy looked down at the nearest typewriter, saw the little correcting button, and turned red. "Oh, God."

"What do you think of the new girl?" Barbara Adams asked Maria and Margaret as they waited for the machine to drop their Cokes.

"I never trusted any broad who wore glasses on her tits," Margaret cackled, "but she's not bad at all. Having a rough time of it though."

"I think she's very sweet," Maria said.

Barbara put a quarter in the machine and pushed a button with her fist. "Oh hell, here comes Lee. She's collecting for something again—"

"Probably Maryann's abortion," Margaret said.

"Lets go." Barbara grabbed her can of Coke and they walked off, passing the table where Violet and Judy were finishing lunch.

"Hi, Judy," Maria said, "how's it going with you?"

"Fine, thanks. Violet's going to show me around outside."

"Yeah," Violet said, "we practically inhaled our lunches. Never wolfed down anything so fast in my life. Hart asked me to pick up a scarf for his wife."

"The nerve," Margaret growled.

Barbara nodded over to the door. Doralee had just entered the lunch room. "Why didn't he ask *her?* She does *everything else* for him."

Margaret put on an imitation of Doralee's accent.

"Oh, the poor thing's too tired. Ya all know they've been in *conference* together all morning."

"Cool it, ladies," Violet said, and she and Judy rose from the table. "So long, and don't forget to put your claws back in their sheaths."

Judy followed Violet out of the room, unable to restrain her curiosity. "Violet, what did Margaret mean about Doralee?"

Violet answered over her shoulder. "Rumor has it that she's banging the boss."

"She and Mr. Hart?"

"Yup."

"I think that's awful."

"Live and let live, I say. Except that, frankly, Judy, I always credited Doralee with more brains. And certainly more taste. I mean, with a man who wears elevator shoes."

"That's how my husband left me."

"In elevator shoes?"

"No. He was having an affair with his secretary."

"I don't think F. Hart's going to leave his wife. Missy's been too good a meal ticket all these years."

"She's got money?"

"Yeah. And she's bananas."

"Bananas? In what way?"

"She adores him," Violet replied.

Hart looked up as Doralee entered "Hold it right there!"

"Where?" she asked, stopping in her tracks.

"Just turn around a second. I want to see something."

She did a twirl; then asked, "Is anything wrong? Something on my dress?"

"It's the something *in* your dress," he quipped.

She closed the door, sighed, walked toward him, and sat in the chair opposite his desk. She opened her pad, folded her legs and gave him a pleasant, business-like smile. "Shall we begin?"

"I want you to take a letter to Vernon Henshaw over at Metropolitan Mutual. 'Dear Vern. As you know, the Chairman of the Board of Consolidated Companies, Mr. Russell Tinsworthy, spends most of his time working on the model city and jungle clearance operation that the Brazilian government asked him to undertake some years ago. Consequently, we here at . . .' " As he spoke, he stole a glance at Doralee to see if she was watching. She wasn't. Hart pushed one of his file folders so that it nudged some books to the edge of his desk. " ' . . . Consolidated would like to set up a meeting with you to discuss the good possibility of a joint venture in the insuring of our company workers in relation to . . .' " He gave the file another shove. The books toppled, taking with them several pencils. "Oops." He rose as if to retrieve them.

"Don't worry," Doralee said, setting down her pad and pencil. "I'll get them." She moved to her knees, affording Hart an ample view of her more than ample bosom. He rushed around the desk to assist her. "Here, let me help."

"I've got them. It's okay." Doralee started to get up.

Hart knelt in front of her, and grasped her arm. "Doralee," he said tensely.

"Yes?"

"About my conduct in the office yesterday. I got carried away. I'd like to apologize."

"That's all right, Mr. Hart. I've been chased by swifter men than you, and I haven't been caught yet." She pulled her arm away. "Shall we get back to the letter now?"

"Come over here," he said, getting up, extending a hand to assist her. "Come over here for just a minute. I have something I want to give you."

They got up and walked to the leather sofa, where they sat under the deer's head sticking out from the wall. "Well, Doralee?" Hart said. "I . . ." He paused for a long time.

"Yes, Mr. Hart?"

"You know, ever since I made that mistake about the convention in San Francisco . . ."

She seemed relieved. "Oh, is that what's bothering you? You didn't make a mistake. I'll just be sure next time when I'm asked to go work a convention, that there is really a convention going on."

"Look, nothing happened, so let's forget it. You mean a lot to me, much more than just a secretary, and"—he reached under the sofa and withdrew a square, flat box with a loose ribbon tied around it—"I bought this especially for you. I even picked it out myself."

"Why, thank you. You didn't have to do that."

"I know." He handed it to her.

Inside the box was a lovely scarf, the very one Violet had bought during her lunch hour, supposedly for Mrs. Hart. "It's lovely. Thank you."

Hart moved closer to her. "Doralee, look at me. I'm a rich man. I've got a checkbook over there and you could write your own figure."

"I could do that now, Mr. Hart. I sign your name better than you do."

"I'm serious. I'm crazy about you."

"Mr. Hart, I've told you before, I'm a married woman."

"And I'm a married man. That's what makes it so perfect. Oh, Doralee, I love your dimples." He lunged to kiss her, but she fended him off with a raised knee and a fast shove, sort of a country version of a karate chop. They both rolled off the sofa, landing with a double thud on the floor.

Doralee scrambled to her feet. "Mr. Hart, are you all right?"

"Please call me Frank," he groaned.

And, at that moment, someone did. But it wasn't Doralee. "Frank!" Missy Hart asked, "What *are* you doing there on the floor?"

Hart pulled himself up with whatever dignity he could muster. "Eh, nothing, dear," he mumbled, brushing his pant legs. "I . . . tripped. Hit my knee on the coffee table."

"Oh, that's awful." Missy seemed genuinely concerned. "Did you hurt yourself?"

"No." He gave her a peck on the cheek. "What

are you doing down here anyway? I hate it when you come to the office like this."

She smiled. "Oh, Frank, don't be mad at me. I've just come from the travel agency. They have the most wonderful choices for cruises. Hello, Doralee."

"Mrs. Hart," Doralee acknowledged the greeting.

"How are you? What a lovely scarf."

"Thank you." Doralee smiled an all-too-innocent smile. "It's a gift from your husband."

Hart slumped in his chair.

"I'm so glad he *appreciates* you!" Missy exclaimed to Doralee. "And you are *so* attractive."

"That will be all, Doralee," Hart barked, all executive again. "We'll finish that letter later. Now, Missy, what did you want to show me?"

"Just these brochures," Missy fluttered, digging in her Gucci bag. "It won't take but a second."

"Good, 'cause I'm busy."

"Franklin, you know you did promise to go."

"Right, right," Hart said, his eyes on Doralee as she went out the door.

"This is a lovely one," Missy babbled. "An Italian line. Looks just like the 'Love Boat,' doesn't it? Four weeks of wonderful sunshine . . ."

"Four weeks? Did you say *four* weeks?"

"Yes, just think of it!"

"I am thinking of it. Are you out of your mind? You think I'm going to spend four weeks of my life drifting around in circles?"

"But, Frank . . ."

"But Frank, nothing. You ask for orange juice in the morning and you get cappuccino, no thank you. You're not getting me to spend a month of my life on some greaseball tugboat. You wanna go yourself, fine and dandy. But not me."

"Frank, you are simply *incorrigible*."

"Damn right. And proud of it. Now, I'm sorry, but I have work to do." And with that, he threw the brochure into the waste can and reached for the telephone.

"Well, I'll be damned," Violet said to Judy.

"Huh?"

"Look over there." She nodded. Judy looked. Doralee had just stepped out of Hart's office and was straightening her dress. "Just look and see who got paid off for services rendered," Violet muttered.

Judy was astonished. "In the *office?* During *working* hours?"

"No, no, the payoff," Violet said. "Check her neck."

Judy brought her hand to her mouth. "My God. That's the scarf you bought."

Violet shrugged. "What the hell, she must have earned it."

Overhearing, old Margaret barked, "Deserves a lot more, having to sleep with that crumb."

Violet ignored her. "Come on, Judy, I'll bet you can't wait to see the copying room."

"Sure."

After Violet taught Judy how to run the two smaller machines, she explained how to operate the mammoth 8200, but warned Judy to read the manual first.

"Where's the manual?" Judy asked.

Violet pointed to a binder on the shelf. "That's it. Look at it in your spare time."

"I'd need two weeks of vacation—that thing's thicker than *Gone with the Wind*."

"And a lot less exciting. Listen, the thing to know is if anything starts going wrong, just look at the panel. The machine will tell you what to do."

"Okay. I'm sure I can handle it."

"Fine. Now, come back to the desk with me and I'll give you a complete file. We need six copies."

"Right."

Judy got the file and returned to the copying room. She studied the buttons of one of the smaller machines, then tried one page. She inserted the paper, pushed the PRINT button and out came a copy at the other end. After a quick glance at the 8200 Manual, she turned on the big machine. The automatic feeder pulled the pages in and six copies inserted themselves into the collator at the other end.

It worked smoothly until Judy inadvertently hit a button which increased the speed. The copies came out faster and faster, until several of them jammed. Judy moved to sort them by hand, syncronizing herself with the rhythm of the machine . . .

And then, disaster. Everything seemed to go wrong at once.

Judy panicked. She had no idea how to turn the machine off. Trying to catch some flying pages with one hand, she turned the selector dial with the other, hoping to change it from 6 to 0. Somehow, it came out 60, and the machine was suddenly spewing a blizzard of paper around the room. Pages shot from every angle, covering all the equipment and piling up on the floor. Judy smashed her fist at the control panel and CALL KEY OPERATOR flashed in her face.

"Help!" Judy screamed. *"Violet—Key Operator —Someone!"* She knocked a bottle of dry ink to the floor. It burst open and her shoes suddenly turned black. "Help me!"

In a conference room down the hall, Jack Meade and Chuck Strell, both vice presidents of the company, were concluding a long and difficult meeting with Frank Hart.

Meade, the senior of the two, gathered his papers together. "Look, Frank," he snapped, "the way you run your department is your business. All I ask is you keep your nose out of mine."

"Jack, I just made a few suggestions," Hart said. "No reason to get huffy. I'm sorry I said anything."

"So am I." And Meade stormed out.

Strell walked with Hart out into the hallway. "You two squabbling should be on the agenda of our meetings," Strell remarked.

"What he needs is a good piece of ass," Hart retorted.

"Why don't you fix him up with your secretary?"

Strell looked around to see if anyone was listening. "She's the choicest piece around here." He winked broadly.

"No way," Hart said, smugly. "You heard him tell me to keep my nose out of his department. Well, I don't want his nose—or anything else—in mine."

Strell shrugged. "I don't blame you. Not a bad traveling companion to take to a phony convention, right?"

Hart's eyes rolled. "Oh, beautiful. Is that all over the office? Who told you, for God's sake?"

"You did."

"Oh, yeah."

"Hey, Frank, what happened to that cute redhead who worked in Violet's zone?"

"She quit. Some kinda fight with Roz. But her replacement's not bad, if she'd get rid of her glasses. No spring chicken, but I'll bet the meat's still tender."

"You slice it, I'll take something younger. How about that Chinese chick?"

"No way. But there's some dark meat that sits opposite her that may be worth a shot. And then you can always try that fag in the front row."

"Thanks a heap. Hey, have you and Missy decided where you're going on vacation?"

"She's going alone."

"Alone? How come?"

"Wait till you hear what I got planned while she's cruising around the South Seas...." Hart noticed the copying room sign. "Come in here, I'll let you in on it—"

He opened the door.

It was a mistake. The room looked like a wind tunnel for testing the flyability of paper. The astonishing thing was it seemed no one was in the room. Until a hand reached up from behind the 8200, followed by Judy, clenching hundreds of pages to her bosom.

Hart ran to the machine and pressed a button. "What the hell is going on in here?" he shouted.

"I'm sorry, Mr. Hart." Judy looked at Strell. "Are you the Key Operator?"

"What?"

"What's this all about?" Hart demanded.

"It was . . . it was going too fast."

"Too fast! Jesus Christ, couldn't you shut it off?"

"I . . . I didn't know how."

"Didn't know *how*? Shit, it's right here in front of you!" He pointed to the button that said STOP PRINT.

Judy looked at it and said, "Oh."

Strell backed out of the doorway. "Catch you later, Frank. Great little scheme you got here all right."

Hart turned to Judy. "Weren't you checked out on this thing? A moron can operate it."

"I was doing all right. I mean, I was checked out. I know what to do now."

He picked up a sheet of paper. "The Henderson Dynamics file! My God, you'd better get this into shape." He dropped the page despairingly. "I suggest you get to learn these machines backwards and forwards, or your first day in here is going to be your last. Understand?"

"Yes, sir."

"Now, clean this up and get back to work." He stomped out, mumbling a variety of expletives.

By the time Judy emerged, it was closing time. She placed the original file on Violet's desk and put the copies in the mail basket as Violet had instructed. Then, wearily, she made her way back to her desk, sat down, and took a deep breath. The clock hit five and a buzzer sounded. Judy heaved a sigh, grabbed her purse, turned off her typewriter, and made her way with the others toward the elevators.

Down in the time-card room, Margaret, standing behind Judy, said, "Hey, smile, kid. You're on parole."

"Only for a night," Judy answered despairingly.

"Wanna have a drink at Charlie's with me? We'll

celebrate your first day and my nine hundredth year."

"No, thanks Margaret. I'm too tired."

Margaret waved and left. Then, as Judy punched out, Maria saw her and pulled her aside. "Are you okay?"

"Yes. Why?"

"I saw you when you came out of the copying room."

"Oh."

"Judy, you can't ever let them get to you. I have a rule here: *they won't ever make me cry.* They're not worth it. You should make that your motto too."

"I know. It was silly. Believe me, I'll never let it happen again. I'm going to go home, take a warm bath, and forget I ever heard the words CALL KEY OPERATOR again."

In the elevator, Judy remembered what Tom had whispered to her as she passed his desk. "The first day's always the worst." She hoped to hell he was right.

Judy was dreaming of millions of lavender bubbles, bubbles to soak in for hours, as she climbed the stairs to her apartment, one of twenty-six built around the oval swimming pool. A plane flew over, so low Judy thought it would brush the antenna on the roof. She was half-way up the stairs when the roar of the jet vanished, and she realized someone was calling her name.

There he was. Still handsome, still tall, still dressed in jeans and his windbreaker, but no longer her husband. "Dick!" she exclaimed. "What are you doing here?"

He ran up the steps to join her, holding a big envelope under his arm. "I just dropped by to give you these papers. They're the last, the final settlement stuff. You sign them and then give them to your lawyer."

Judy took the envelope. They looked at each other for a long moment, not knowing what to say. Then Judy averted her eyes.

"So how are things with you?" Dick asked.

"Fine, fine," she lied, turning back to him. "Everything is just fine. I've got a job. I'm a secretary now." She faked a smile. She was damned if she would give him the satisfaction of knowing a copying machine had almost taken her life earlier that afternoon. "So how's Liza?"

"Lisa."

"Lisa."

"Fine. She's waiting in the car. We've got to go." Dick looked at her—was he thinking of kissing her?—and then put out his hand, awkwardly.

Judy shook it. Then she watched him bound down the stairs, leap the back of the diving board, and hurry out the front gate. She shrugged and continued up to her apartment, once again fantasizing of soothing bubbles, putting all thoughts of Dick and the office out of her mind.

Three

"Vi, would you look at this?" Bob Enright pointed to a bill on his desk. "I've checked all over and I can't make it out." He handed it to her.

She read it. "Ajax Warehouse. But we don't deal with any Ajax Warehouse . . . at least I don't think we do."

"That's what I thought."

"Hmmm." Violet pulled the pencil from her hair and made a note to herself on a piece of scratch paper on Bob's desk, then clipped it to the bill. "I'll have to track this one down."

"Thanks, Vi."

Violet headed back to her section where Judy was typing inventory reports, and moaning every time she had to add the figures.

"You want them to buy you a computer, honey?" Betty called out. "Hell, they won't even get me a new cushion for my chair, let alone a computer. My tush has had the same spring goosing me now for what's going on two years."

"Truth is," Tom piped up, "the company has three floors of computers. They just like to keep us at a certain torture level."

"Boy," Judy put in, "they sure know how to do it to me." She took her hands away from the keys and turned to Tom. "Listen, I never thought to ask, and I haven't been able to figure it out from anything I've worked on. What exactly does Consolidated do?"

"Do?"

30

"I mean what kind of business is it, really?"

Tom shrugged. "Slavedriving."

Judy persisted. "No, I mean the actual—" She was cut off by the lunch bell, followed by an immediate exodus of her co-workers.

Judy headed to her locker in the kitchen and took out the sandwich she'd made the night before. Worried she might forget it in her rush to get to work on time, she had put it in her purse and stuck her purse in the refrigerator for the night. The cold lipstick had been somehow refreshing on the drive into town, but the sandwich was slightly soggy.

Margaret opened her locker and took out her lunch—a hip flask, which she uncorked without a sound, and placed to her mouth. When she realized Judy was staring at her, Margaret pulled the flask away from her face and whispered, "For medicinal purposes. I have to keep my sanity."

As Judy headed back to her desk, she wondered how long it would take office life to get her to the point where she'd keep her locker stocked with scotch. Her reverie was interrupted by Doralee. "Hello, Judy. How's it going?"

"Fine, thanks."

"Say, would you like to have lunch with me today? I'm a little late. Mr. Hart kept me on the phone all morning, booking his wife's trip. I'm about four hours behind in my regular work, but I'm famished."

"No, thanks, Doralee. I'm afraid I can't . . . um . . . anyway, I already grabbed a sandwich."

"Well, maybe tomorrow. There's the cutest little Italian place just a hop, skip and a jump from here." Doralee giggled. "I guess I have it on my mind because I've been talking to an Italian cruise-ship line all morning."

"Thanks," Judy said, "but I'm going to stay around the office for a while. Get to know the routine. Thanks anyway."

"Oh, yeah, sure," Doralee said, and quickly turned away.

Judy wondered whether she'd hurt Doralee's feelings. She hoped she hadn't, but she just couldn't con-done Doralee's actions with her boss, and that was that. Besides, what would Judy's new friends think if she were to begin palling around with Doralee? No, Doralee was off limits, and it wasn't up to Judy to break the ground rules.

Doralee sat at her dressing table brushing her shining blonde hair, humming a country song. Dwayne leaned back against the pillows propped against the bed's velvet, heart-shaped headboard, and watched his wife concernedly. "What's the matter, honey pie?" he asked.

"I'm as nice as can be down at that office, and still everyone treats me like a bastard at a family reunion."

"Forget about them, baby," Dwayne drawled, stretching his arms and then folding them over his chest. "Come on to bed. I'll give you a warm reception."

"I'll bet you will."

"Come here, sugar plum."

She crawled into the bed next to his lanky frame. "I don't get it, Dwayne. They all give me the cold shoulder."

"I've got a warm shoulder for you."

She bit it. "Mmm. You've got more than a shoulder."

"You can say that again." He turned to face her. "I don't like to see you upset. I don't like it one bit."

"Oh, I'm all right. I've got you, don't I?"

"You sure as hell do." He kissed her on the lips, gently, softly. "But don't you miss the life in the rodeo and all that attention and whatnot?"

She shook her head. "We came here to get away from that. I know you're much happier here with a real chance to show your talent. I mean, you're singing all over town now. It's just a matter of time till some producer hears you and signs you up."

"But are *you* happy? At that office?"

"Of course. I love the job, I really do. I just wish I had some friends down there. It gets lonely."

He hugged her tight. "Just you wait, when I make my first million, I'm gonna *buy* you that Consolidated place."

She curled up in his arms. "When you do, be sure to fire Mr. Hart and make me your secretary."

"Just wait, honey, things are gonna be great one day, for both of us. . . ."

"Dwayne, I don't have to wait. I've got all a girl could ever want to have right here and now."

He kissed her again. "You sure as hell do." And then he reached out and clicked off the lamp.

"Is he in?"

"Yes, Violet, just a sec." Doralee punched the intercom. "Mr. Hart, Violet would like to see you."

"Yeah, all right, send her—" Doralee cut him off. "Go on in, Violet."

"Thanks." Violet entered Hart's office, and handed him the bill that Bob Enright had given her the day before.

"What's this?"

"A bill."

"I can see it's a bill, Violet. But what *about* this bill?"

"That's what I've been trying to figure out, Mr. Hart."

He read it. "Ajax Warehouse. What about it?"

"We know nothing about it here. I've called everywhere, Los Angeles, Chicago, even New York, but of course, they're all tied up with planning that computer changeover, no one could give me a definite answer."

"Hmmm." He rubbed his chin. "Let me look into this. I think Mr. Hinkle upstairs was talking about it." He set the bill on a pile of papers on his desk. "Anything else?"

"Well, I was wondering about the report I did on the color coding of accounts. I gave it to you last month. I'm sure if you just looked over the research and the studies, you'd see we could improve efficiency by up to twenty percent."

"Color coding?" He looked blank for a moment. "Yes, yes, oh, now I remember. I looked at it."

She waited for an answer.

He just sat there smiling at her.

"Well, what did you think of it?"

"I thought it needed work. I'll get back to you on it."

She held her breath, counted to ten, then turned and marched out.

Violet swept by Doralee, muttering, "He's a jerk, nothing but a jerk. . . ." As she headed for the women's washroom.

After checking under the stalls and finding no feet, Violet let out what might have been described as a primal scream. Slightly relieved, she splashed water on her face and returned to her office.

Roz Keith was waiting for the executive elevator. "Hello, Violet. Did you get my memo?"

"Yes, I did, Roz. I *tore* right through it."

"Good!" Roz exclaimed. "We must clamp down hard on any signs of unionization, keep our ears open for people sharing their complaints or revealing their salaries."

"Why don't we just avoid the problem by paying everyone the same salary for the same work?"

"Really, Violet, sometimes I think you're out of touch." Roz looked over Violet's shoulder. "Here comes Mr. Hart with Mr. Hinkle."

Violet turned and saw Chester Hinkle, President of Consolidated, who walked, talked, and dressed with full knowledge of that fact. "Hello, girls," he boomed. "How's it going?"

"Just fine," Violet said, flatly.

"Oh, Roz," Hinkle said, "you'll be getting a copy of this report Frank has just given me. We're going to start color coding the accounts from now on. Frank's done a brilliant study of its efficiency."

Hart beamed. "Thank you, sir."

Violet looked as if she'd just been struck by a club.

"That does sound fine," Roz said. "Congratulations, Mr. Hart."

"Thanks," Hart said, avoiding Violet's glare. The elevator arrived and he and Hinkle stepped in.

But Hinkle put his hand on the doors and said, "Yes, it's just a *brilliant* idea. You're a fine piece of manpower, Frank. Any other reforms you want to do down here are fine with me. This is your floor. You run it as you please. Going up, girls?"

"No," Violet said, pointedly. "We're going *down.*"

"I can't believe that man," Violet moaned. It was evening and she and her sixteen-year-old son, Josh, were installing a garage-door opener at home. Violet was standing on a ladder, putting in the last screws, while Josh patiently listened to his mother's harangue. "He has no shame, Josh! None! Stood right there and presented my idea to the president of the company as if it was his own."

"So why didn't you call him on it?"

Violet turned a screw tight. "Because I'm playing it safe, dammit. In six weeks he's making the decision on the promotion, so I'll keep on playing the 'good girl' until then." She put her arms down and waited to see if the apparatus would fall on her head. It didn't.

"You finished up there?" Josh asked.

"Yeah."

"Nice job."

"Thanks." She came down from the ladder. "Can you imagine? A mature woman with four kids who can install a garage-door opener and he still refers to me as his 'girl?' "

"Sounds like a real asshole, Ma."

"Watch your language. But yes, he is." She clenched her fists. "God, he makes me crazy!"

Josh pointed his finger at her. "Mum, what you need is to relax. I'm going to roll you a joint."

"Now, wait a minute, Josh, you know my feelings

about that. Your grandmother goes into fits at the very mention of marijuana." She pointed out through the garage window. Her mother was sitting in a lawn chair, talking to Violet's oldest daughter, Laurie. "Josh, you don't want to hurt that dear old woman who loves you, do you?"

"Ma, Granny doesn't understand moderation. 'Harm springs from excess,' right?"

"Yes . . . but I don't know. . . ."

"Sometimes I think Granny needs a toke once in a while herself."

"Josh!"

"Ma, we're talking one joint. Uno."

"Yes, but . . ."

"Ma, how long have you been waiting for that promotion?"

Violet leaned against the ladder. "Slip it into my purse."

Violet learned the news in Hart's office. When he told her his decision, she thought she hadn't heard him correctly. Then she thought he was kidding. Then she jumped up and screamed, "What? How *dare* you!"

Hart kept his desk between them. "Let me finish. Let me finish, Violet."

"Finish? I'm the one who's finished."

"Don't fly off the handle—"

But Violet would not be assuaged. "You gave that promotion to Bob Enright instead of me? I've got five years' seniority over him! Every problem with his section, he still comes to me for help. For Christ's sake, *I* trained him!"

"Look, the company feels—"

"The company, bullshit! It's *your* decision. *You* promoted him." She narrowed her eyes and glared at him. "Just tell me why."

"Well . . . in the first place, he's got a college degree."

"Oh, brilliant. While he was in college getting his

precious, useless degree, I was working my butt off for this company."

"He's got a family to support," Hart argued.

She was seething. "And I don't?" She turned her head and bit her lip to keep from going completely berserk. Then she said, "Anyway, what's that got to do with anything?"

"Look," Hart pleaded, "my hands are tied. I need a *male* in that position. Clients prefer to deal with a man when it comes to figures."

She nodded, slowly up and down. "Now we're getting at it. I lose a promotion because of some idiot prejudice. The boys in the club are threatened by any woman who doesn't want to sit in the back of the bus."

"Spare me that women's lib crap. I see you're upset about this and I understand it." He pulled at his mustache nervously.

"You understand *nothing*."

He walked in front of his chair, putting his hands on his desk, bending forward a little. "I understand I'm still the boss here, and though you might be pretty valuable out there, you had better get a hold of yourself, because I'm not going to sit here and take this." And he sat down heavily. So heavily, the whole chair tipped back and ejected him onto the floor.

Flustered as she'd never seen him before, Hart pulled himelf to his feet and pressed the button on the intercom. "Goddammit, Doralee, get in here. I told you to fix my chair six weeks ago." He took his hand from the button and rubbed his elbow.

"Okay," Violet said, "I'll leave, but I have one more thing to say before I go. Don't you *ever* refer to me as your 'girl' again. I'm sick and tired of hearing 'my girls' this and 'our girls' that."

Doralee entered and stood near the door.

"What in God's name are you talking about?" Hart barked.

"I didn't say a word," Doralee explained.

"Not you. *Her!*"

"I'll tell you what I'm talking about," Violet said firmly. "I'm no girl. I'm a *woman*. W–O–M–A–N!" She pointed a long finger at Hart. "I'm not your wife, I'm not your mother, or even"—she turned to point her finger at Doralee—"your mistress. I am your *employee*," the decibels in Violet's voice escalated, "and as such I expect to be treated equally, with dignity and respect!"

"What do you mean, 'mistress'?" Doralee choked.

Violet barked, "Oh, come off it, Doralee. The whole company knows you two are having an affair."

Hart was turning purple. "Don't pay any attention to her," he warned Doralee. "She's upset, she's ... she's crazy."

"What?" Doralee screamed. "The whole company? Since when?"

"I don't know," Violet shouted back. "Since your weekend together in San Francisco."

Hart said, "Violet, I think you'd better go."

"No, wait a danged minute, Violet," Doralee ordered. "It's not true. Who told you about San Francisco? Who's been saying we're having an affair?"

"Who's been saying it?" Violet laughed out loud. She pointed to Hart. *"He* has!" And with that, she stormed out, slamming the door so hard behind her, the glass shook.

Violet swept past Margaret, who looked up at her. "Hey, Violet, where are you goin'?"

"I'm going to get drunk."

Margaret nodded. "Atta girl!"

Hart backed up as Doralee stalked him around the desk. "You've been telling everybody I'm sleeping with you! That explains it, why everyone treats me like some ten-cent floozie." She quickened her pace as he retreated. "They all think I'm screwing the boss!"

"No! No!" he protested. "It's not like that at all."

She lowered her voice. "And you love it, don't you? It gives you some sort of cheap thrill. Like knocking over pencils and picking up papers." She swung out and spilled his pencils all over the room and then swept every last paper from his desk.

He grabbed her hand. "Doralee, don't get yourself all excited. . . ."

"Keep your grimy hands off me!" She pulled away. "I have been straight with you from the first day I came here. And you—"

"Can't we sit down and discuss this?"

"Where? On the sofa? Well, of course on the sofa, now that you don't even have a chair left." She clenched her fists. "I've put up with your pinching, your ogling, your gifts, and your chasing me around the desk because I need this job, but this is the last straw." Her eyes turned beady, her voice grim. "You know, I've got a gun in my purse out there. . . ."

He gulped. "Doralee, dear, there's no reason to get all hysterical."

"Up to now I've been forgiving and forgetting because of the way I was brought up, but I'll tell you one thing, if you ever—*ever*—say another word about me or make another indecent proposal, I'm going to get that gun of mine and change you from a rooster to a hen with one shot!" She looked him in the eye, her face only inches from his, and yelled. "AND DON'T THINK I CAN'T DO IT!"

Doralee, with her purse and coat, shoved past Roz, who was on her way to see Hart. "Where are you going?" Roz called to her.

"I'm taking the rest of the day off. And right now, I need a drink."

Margaret looked up from her desk and nodded again. "Atta girl!" she snorted.

Hart was picking pencils and papers off his floor, next to his wrecked chair, when Roz entered. "What the hell do *you* want?" he snarled. "Can't you see I'm busy?"

She closed the door behind her. "I wouldn't bother you if this wasn't important. But I've just heard one of the girls commit a serious infraction."

Annoyed, he mumbled, "What are you talking about?"

"Maria Delgrado was in the ladies room, speaking to some other girl whose voice I couldn't recognize, when I distinctly overheard her reveal her salary and make estimates of yours and mine."

Hart was reaching for a pencil way under his desk. "Well, get rid of her. Dismiss her."

"It's not that she hasn't been warned," Roz continued. "I clearly outlined it in my memo, which—"

"Didn't you hear what I said?" he shouted, up on his knees now. "Fire the bitch."

Roz blinked. "Yes, sir."

A security guard watched as Maria, desperately trying not to break into tears, cleared out her desk.

Judy, who had been in the copying room, returned as Maria emptied her last drawer. "Maria got sacked," Margaret said. "Roz heard her talkin' shop in the can. Ratted on her to Hart."

"What? I don't believe it. She was fired for *talking?*"

"About salary. That's one of Roz's pressure points, the old cow."

"It's all right, Judy," Maria said. "I wanted to spend more time with my kids anyhow."

"But it's so unfair," Judy said. "We've got to do something."

"Yeah," Margaret bellowed. "Let's all revolt."

"This place *needs* a revolution," Tom said.

"No!" Maria cried. "Don't you get into any trouble. It's not worth it. I'll find another job. It's hard for me to work full time anyway." Tears were streaming down her round cheeks. "I'm sorry. I promised myself I wouldn't cry."

Judy's voice was angry now. "Where's Violet? Does she know about this?"

"Not yet," Margaret answered. "She's down at Charlie's getting drunk." Margaret looked as if she wanted to add, "And that's what we all should be doing."

"Well, I'm going to tell her," Judy announced. "If anyone wants me, I'll be at the bar around the corner." She grabbed her purse and stormed off.

"Atta girl!" Margaret shouted.

Four

"What a rat," Violet said.

"What a liar," Doralee chimed in.

"What a creep," Judy added.

All three were working on their third round of drinks at Charlie's Bar.

Doralee murmured slowly and softly, "To think he told everyone I was sleeping with him."

"To do that to Maria," Judy moaned. "It's so unfair."

"Twelve years of service and he shoots me down." Violet downed the rest of her drink.

"Well, we have to *do* something," Judy said, decisively. "He can't treat people like that."

"Do?" Violet asked. "What's to do? Quit?"

"I can't quit," Doralee said. "Not until my husband gets his career going."

Violet shook her head. "It's the same all over anyway. The Harts of this world run offices everywhere."

"Couldn't we all get together and complain to Hinkle?" Judy asked.

"Complain to Hinkle?" Doralee laughed. "He's as bad as Hart. Besides, they're tight as thieves."

"Yeah," Violet moaned, "Hinkle loves his color coding. Let's face it. We're in a pink-collar ghetto." Only ice was left in her glass. "So let's have another drink."

Judy motioned the bartender. "This round's on me."

"No, no, no," Violet objected, opening her purse. "I've got it this time." She looked inside and a grin creased her face. "Oh, my," she said, "I've *really* got it." She pulled out the joint that Josh had rolled for her weeks ago.

"What's that?" Judy asked.

"I never saw you smoke," Doralee said. "You roll your own?"

"A little present from my son. Say, why don't we just skip over to the ladies' room and light it?"

Doralee leaned over and sniffed. "Violet, that's marijuana!"

"Shh!" Violet put it back in her purse. "Come on."

Judy grabbed Violet's hand. "I don't think we should. What if someone came in?"

Doralee cautioned, "It's awful dangerous."

"Would you two show a little spunk?" Violet snapped. "What are you anyway, men or mice?" She giggled. "I mean women or mice?"

"Why don't we go to my place," Doralee suggested. "Dwayne's out on a gig tonight and we'll have it all to ourselves."

"Okay by me," Violet said. "We'll have an old-fashioned female pot party." She laughed and then whispered, "Oh, my boy will be *so* proud."

They got up from the bar stools just as the bartender approached them. Judy shook her head at him. Doralee said, "To tell the truth, girls, it doesn't do that much for me."

"Me too," Judy added. "I smoked some grass at a party once. I could never understand what the big deal was."

"Well, Josh raves about it. But whenever I've warned him about it, he tells me, 'Ma, one joint now and then, what's the big deal? One joint can't even make you high.' Well, what the hell, at least I'll be able to say I tried it once."

They marched out together, a little unsteadily, but together.

They were stretched out around the fireplace on the floor of Doralee's family room, giggling like crazy. Doralee was giving them a blow-by-blow account of her run-in with Hart. ". . . and I told him I had a gun in my purse and the next time he tried to put his clammy hands on me, I'd shoot him where it mattered."

Judy shrieked with laughter. "Oh, oh God, that's funny. Threatening Hart with a gun!"

"He knows I have one too," Doralee insisted.

"You do not," Judy said.

"Look, right here." She pulled the gun from her purse on the Barcalounger and showed them.

"My heavens," Judy said, "you really do have a gun!"

Violet put her head back on the floor and squealed. "Oh, he must have been ready to crap in his drawers!"

"Have you ever fired it?" Judy was amazed.

"Only once. Right after Dwayne bought it for me, my girlfriend and I were coming back late at night from a rodeo in Dallas. Two guys started hassling us in the parking lot."

"Two *Harts,* you mean," Violet piped in.

"Yup," Doralee agreed. "Real jerks. They wouldn't quit, so I reached for the gun and shot a bullet right through my purse." Violet and Judy convulsed. Doralee jumped up and ran to a closet filled with brooms and old towels and cleaning supplies. "I still have that purse." She reached up and yanked down a white straw handbag with a hole in it, complete with powder burns. "See." Judy and Violet were gasping for breath. "It did the trick, though. They ran off."

"I'll bet they did," Violet said, pounding the floor with her hands. "An exploding purse!"

Judy took another drag on the joint. "This is good put. I mean pot. My God, I can't even talk straight. What did you call it again?"

Violet giggled. "Maui Wowie!"

Judy closed her eyes and let out her breath.

"Well, I love it. Just love it." She passed the joint to Doralee, who sat down again.

"I don't think I could ever carry a gun," Violet mused. "I could never understand those guys like Hart who go out in the woods to hunt those poor, defense-less animals like Bambi and Thumper and that cute little skunk."

"I'd like to hunt Hart," Doralee growled. "Chase his lily white tail through the woods and see how he likes it."

Judy collapsed in a fit of hilarity, squirming on the floor, grabbing a pillow and putting it over her face to quiet herself down.

Violet and Doralee looked at teach other. "I think she's stoned," Violet said, and then laughed hysterical-ly herself. "Chase his tail through the woods . . . oh, Lord!"

Judy pulled the pillow off her mouth. "Am I stoned?" she asked, gazing at the ceiling.

Doralee confirmed it. "You're stoned."

"I'm stoned!" Judy shouted and tossed the pillow into the air. "Oh, that's so funny."

"What's so funny?" Doralee asked.

"I just had this image of Hart, running for his life through a jungle. The warriors are after him with torches and clubs and elephant guns . . . hah! A big game hunt, and everyone who's hunting him works at the office."

Violet shrieked. "Betty and Tom and Margaret, the whole gang, out hunting Hart like some escaped convict!"

Judy sat up. "Friends and countrymen," she said, "Lend me your ears and I'll tell you the story of the mob and the monster." With that, Judy lurched to her feet, and assured of Violet and Doralee's full attention said, "Now, picture this . . ."

It was night.
The hungry mob moved through the streets of the *city, carrying torches and a hangman's noose. They*

were led by a pack of vicious, barking bloodhounds. This was the notorious and deadly gang of C.C. employees, names as feared today as Jesse James and Jack the Ripper in their times. Barbara "The Barbarian" Adams. Betty "Killer" Stokes. The dread Charlotte Whitherspoon and Lee "The Collector" Chang. Margaret Foster, also known as "Margie The Lush." Maria Delgrado with a vengeance. Tom "Madman" Wood. Eddie Smith with his lethal, metal-spiked mailcart. Jack "Monster" Meade.

The gang entered the building. They smashed their way in through the front windows. They knew he was in there. In there hiding. And they were going to get him once and for all.

They made their way to the sixteenth floor. It was hot. The air conditioning was not on. But it didn't deter them. The hounds picked up his scent. They found traces of his mad dash along the main aisle—a file knocked over, a chair kicked sideways. They searched the desks and corridors of offices. Not a waste can was left unturned. Revenge burned in their blood. And the oppressive night air bristled with impending doom.

Suddenly, there was a shout. Mad Maria saw him and screamed, "THERE HE IS!"

Sure enough. The light from the torches illuminated the figure of a man crouching in terror behind a desk in the corner of the huge room. Franklin Hart was breathing heavily and sweating like a cornered rat.

"Get him!" Monster Meade shouted.

"Get the bastard!" Margie The Lush barked.

Hart made a dash for the elevators, but Charlotte —all two hundred pounds of her—was coming around the bend fast, heading him off. He turned and ran down the center aisle, then leaped one desk, two, three. Luck was on his side. It was dark in that corner. He slowly and quietly opened the door to his office and entered. He closed it but for an inch or two, and crouching, watched the crazed mob rush by.

The shouting and barking receded into the distance. Hart stood up, brushing himself off. Thank God, he was safe. He wiped his brow, took a handkerchief from his suit-coat pocket and dabbed at his mustache. Then he turned around—and froze.

Someone was in the room with him.

At first he just sensed it, that sick sensation when you know something isn't the way you'd like it to be and there's nothing you can do but confront it. As his eyes adjusted to the light coming from the street windows, he made out a figure sitting in his chair, behind his desk. But the shadows were against him. He couldn't distinguish the face. "Who's there?" *he asked.*

The stranger moved a hand ever so slowly to the desk, to the base of the lamp Missy had bought for him the day he'd been promoted to vice president. The fingers jumped and the light flicked on. Judy Bernly sat there, eyes peering through the harsh light, eyes filled with anticipation. She was dressed as a big-game hunter.

"Hello, Hart."

He said nothing. Only gulped.

"It looks like you've gotten yourself into a spot of trouble."

"Judy," *he panted, ringing his hands together.* "You've got to help me. That mob out there has gone crazy. They're trying to—" *He could barely say it.*

"Spit it out, boss."

"They're trying to kill me."

Judy looked perplexed. "Why should they do a nasty thing like that?"

"I don't know," *he whined.* "I'm not such a bad guy."

"You're a sexist, egotistical, lying, hypocritical bigot."

"So I have a few faults. Who doesn't? Is that any reason to kill someone?"

She stood up. She looked like she was on a safari. She paced up and down, taking long, heavy strides, pondering the situation as if she were in the bush and this was a life/death decision. "I'm going to give you a break, Hart. A break that you wouldn't give one of those people out there."

"Judy," he begged, hearing shouts in the background again, his hands together as if praying, "hide me until they go away."

"I'm going to count to ten," Judy said, methodically, without any visible emotion. "Then I'm coming after you myself."

He was stunned. "You can't mean that."

She glared at him.

He knew she meant it. "But, Judy—"

"You're foul, Hart. A wart on the nose of humanity." She picked up the hunting rifle which was sitting on his desk and spun it a couple of times around her head with the skill of a crack marksman. Then she pointed it in the direction of his nostrils. "And I'm going to blast it off," she snarled.

He cried out for his life. "Judy! Judy! Judy!"

"Good-bye, boss man." She cocked the rifle. "It's gettin' to be quittin' time for you."

He backed away. "You can't mean this. . . ."

She started the countdown. "One. Two. Three—"

"But why me? I'm just an ordinary guy trying to do a decent job."

"Four. Five. Six—"

He put his arm out and waved the flat of his hand to the side a few times. "Okay, so I'm a little pushy, but I wouldn't hurt *anybody.*"

"Seven. Eight. Nine—"

"Holy shit." He saw her take aim. She really was going to blow him away!

"Ten." She fired, blasting the glass out of the door just as he ran out of the room.

Crouching low, he sprinted down the aisle. Judy couldn't see him, but she knew about where he was, so she blasted away at everything in his vicinity. The rifle picked off a typewriter here, a telephone there, cleared a desk of rubber stamps and blew out the screen of a word processor. Hart scurried from the protection of one desk to another. But Judy seemed to have an *inexhaustible supply of ammunition. She shot a lamp and another typewriter.*

Hart ran to the wall, stood smack against it, trying to decide which way to run, and then dropped to his knees as she blasted a hole into the plaster where his head had been.

He darted for the elevator, but Judy was too fast. She stalked him. Rounded the corner. Blasted the Up and Down buttons right off the panel before he could get his hand there. Sparks shot out from the wall.

Hart ran to the stairs. He opened the door and descended, down one flight, then another, and another, and another. He was dizzy from turning corners. His pulse was racing. He was afraid he'd have a heart attack.

Then, there she was, shooting up at him from the landing below. He reversed his direction and went back up, flight after flight, until he reached the sixteenth floor again, the territory he knew better than any other. Where to hide? Ah, where would someone else hide, faced with the same predicament? How about . . . how about Roz? Where would Roz hide?

He ducked into the ladies' room. Panting, he locked himself into the last stall, crossing his legs on the toilet.

And then he heard the door open.

The lights went on, all the bright fluorescent fixtures hidden in the luminous ceiling. Hart sat shaking in fear as he heard her kick open the door to the first stall. Then the second. Then the third. And then—he locked his. Just in time. He was in the fourth.

But that didn't stop Judy Bernly's heavy boot. She kicked the door off its hinges and flattened Hart up against the wall behind the toilet.

They were face to face. The showdown. She brought the rifle into position. It pointed at the spot between his eyes. He held his breath. The tip of the rifle began to lower, down to his mustache, down to his throat, down to his chest and directly at his heart.

And then she pulled the trigger.

EPILOGUE

Judy Bernly rested on the sofa in the office of former vice president, Franklin Hart, Junior, calmly cleaning her rifle. Above her, where the stag head used to hang, she had made a decorating change. She'd had the stuffed deer's head removed, and replaced it with the stuffed head of her former boss.

"I could die!" Violet squealed, in a fit of laughter. "I could just *die!* Good old F. Hart, forever hung on the wall."

"Holy Moses," Doralee said, her ribs aching from laughing, "that's the funniest thing I've ever heard. You should be a writer!"

Judy smiled. "I have to admit, it wasn't bad, huh? God, when you let your imagination run away with him—"

"With *him?*" Violet roared.

"I mean with *you.*" Judy shook her head and sank back to the floor. "I'm stoned, what can I say?"

"Well, I'm hungry," Doralee said. "Talk of a big-game hunt made me starving for some big game."

"Got any?" Violet asked.

"Couple of chicken legs left over from last night." Before they laughed, Doralee waved her finger at them. "But they're *big* chicken legs, the only kind Dwayne likes. Real Southern fried too."

"Mmmm." Judy's eyes brightened. "We haven't had dinner."

"We *drank* dinner," Violet quipped.

"And it was delicious," Doralee added. "But I'm famished." She got up. "Come on, ladies. Let's see what we can whip up."

The dining-room table was soon covered with the results of a refrigerator raid. A case of the "munchies" hit them strong the minute they smelled the food, and they carted out everything that was edible but didn't require cooking. Four chicken legs, a pasta salad, two bags of sour cream and onion potato chips and a jar of pickles disappeared quickly. Violet went back to the meat drawer. "What's for dessert?" She pulled out a salami and grabbed a jar of mayonnaise.

"Yummy," Judy said, as she slopped a gob of mayo onto a slice of the meat.

"Dwayne made the chicken," Doralee explained. "He's a real down-home cook. Makes the best chili. Listen, we got some frozen. I could heat it up."

"Mmm," Judy nodded. "Everything tastes so wonderful. I can't get over it."

Doralee yanked a Tupperware container from the crying-out-to-be-defrosted freezer section, opened it, and shook the frozen lump of chili into a pan. "Best chili you ever tasted. Real Texas style." She turned the gas to high and the pan sizzled.

Violet was eating a pickle wrapped in a potato chip. "Hey, Doralee, how about you?"

"How about me, what?"

"Judy told us her fantasy about doing Hart in. How about you? Don't you have one?"

Doralee turned and leaned against the stove. "I'd like to come riding up one day and give him a taste of his own medicine."

"Riding up?" Judy asked.

"Just like on the ranch, on a palomino. Take care of the varmint like they used to in the Old West."

Violet snickered. "Let's hear it."

"Oh, I don't know. . . ."

"I told you mine," Judy reminded her. "It's your turn. Speech. Bravo, speech!" She clapped her hands and turned her chair to face Doralee.

Spatula in hand, Doralee gestured broadly. "Well, let's see. . . ."

The white horse came riding out of the West.
It passed the corral gates and pulled up short by the hitching post. A cowgirl stepped off, pulled up her white leather gloves, smoothed her fringed skirt, and hurried toward the door leading to the private office.

Who was this wonder from Dodge City, sporting a six-shooter on her hip? Dale Evans? Annie Oakley? Belle Starr?

No. It was Doralee Rhodes. And she had come to town to get the infamous Frank Hart.

She entered the room, striding over to Hart's desk, and sat herself down in his chair. Taking off her gloves, she pressed down the button on the intercom and shouted into the box. "Hey, hot stuff. Grab a pad and pencil and bring your buns in here."

Frank Hart, sitting at the secretary's desk in the outer office, listened to the voice and suddenly became flustered. When she talked like that, there was no telling what was going to happen. He pressed his button and said, sweetly, "Yes, ma'am." *Then he grabbed his pencil and steno pad, checked his tie and hair in the mirror, and realized he couldn't go in looking like* that. *He set the pad and pencil down and tucked the tails of his shirt deep into his pants. Then he gave a last minute check. He licked his fingers and matted down his cowlick. He made sure his fly was closed. Then he picked up the pad and pencil again and went into the office.*

Doralee looked up as he entered, a curious smile on her face. "Just a minute," *she called.* "Stop right there."

"Is anything wrong?" *He pressed his knees together. Was his fly open?*

"There's nothing wrong," *she cooed.* "I just want to check out your bod."

He blushed.

"Turn around a second."

Frank twirled around.

"You know, you got a nice ass, Frank."

He thought he was going to die.

"But you ought to get your pants cut a little tighter." *She pointed.* "Bring it up more in the crotch."

Embarrassed to death, he whispered, "Oh, Mrs. Rhodes."

"I mean you got a nice package, Frank, let's show it off."

He didn't realize it, but he was holding his steno pad directly in front of his zipper.

But, time for business. "Come on over here," she ordered. "I want you to take a memo."

He sat down on the chair facing the desk, crossed his legs, and opened his pad.

Doralee stood up and walked around as she dictated. " 'To All Personnel: I have received some complaints lately about the arrangement of desks and the blank, colorless nature of the office layout.' That's a great cologne you're wearing, Frank." She sniffed the air around him.

"Thank you."

"It's really turning me on. What's it called?"

"I don't know." He didn't sound convincing.

"Sure you do." She swatted him on the back, as if he were "one of the boys." "Don't be embarrassed. What's it called, honey pie?"

"Stud."

"Stud?"

He nodded, his face beet-red. "Stud."

She ran her hand through his hair. "I think it's very sexy." He pulled away a little and she looked down at him with her wide, expressive eyes. "But I don't like that tie, Frankie. What happened to the ones I gave you?"

"Nothing. I just—"

"Take it off."

"What?"

"Take it off! I can't work with those stripes blazing out in living color like that." She put her hands on her hips, looking at him as though he were a perfect idiot. "Good grief. Don't you have any taste?"

He unknotted the tie as hurriedly as he could.

"And unbutton that shirt . . ."

He opened his shirt.

"There, that's better. Now, where were we?"

"The memo."

"Oh, yes, let me see. . . ." She suddenly remembered something and snapped her fingers. "By the way, Frank, I've got a little surprise for you."

"You do?"

She opened her top desk drawer. *"Right in here. Take a look."*

He stood up and leaned over the desk. *"Where?"*

She used her pencil to open his shirt farther and take a gander at his body. *"Hmm. You got a nice lot of hair on your chest,"* she purred. *"How are your pecs?"*

"Mrs. Rhodes, please!" Frank exclaimed. *"I'm a married man. I don't think you should be saying those things to me."*

"Forget about your wife, Frank," Doralee warned. *"She may be yours in the evening, but you're my boy from nine to five. Here, look what I've got for you."* She took a box from the desk drawer and brought it around to him. She opened it carefully, teasing him, making a production out of it, and then pulled out a Western scarf and dangled it in front of his nose. *"Is that not the prettiest thing you ever saw?"*

"Yes. But, Mrs. Rhodes, you shouldn't be buying me gifts. It isn't right."

She ignored his plea. *"Let me put it on you."* She began to put her arms around his neck.

"No . . ."

But she wrapped the scarf around his neck and tied it with a Western knot, being sure to brush the flat of her hand against the stubble of his beard. *"Now, that wasn't so bad, was it?"*

"No," he admitted, nervously.

But she didn't move away. Instead, she ran her fingers through his hair again. *"Mmmm,"* she moaned. She took off her gloves. *"I love your hair, Frank,"* she said, caressing his head, *"so thick, dark, so sexy . . ."*

He jumped up. *"Please, I—"*

She pinched him on the ass. *"And such a cute little tush!"*

"Mrs. Rhodes!"

"Come on, Frank, let's be friendly." She moved closer. He stepped back. *"You've got to be a bit more cooperative if you want to keep this job."*

"Mrs. Rhodes, I've told you, I am not that kind of boy."

"Get off it, Frank." She grabbed him and wrapped her arms about him, pressing her bosom to his still-unbuttoned shirt. "Just a little kiss," she moaned. "No one will ever know. Just one kiss and we'll ride off into the sunset together. The two of us, Frank, back in the saddle again . . ."

He turned his head. "No, no. I won't. I won't." He broke away and ran to the door.

"Frank, you get back here!" she shouted, angry.

He held the door knob and looked at her. "Mrs. Rhodes, I beg you. . . ."

"Frank," she drawled, pointing to the spot right next to her, "come over here."

He didn't move a muscle.

"Frank, I'm warning you. Come over here right now."

He opened the door and made a break for it.

But Doralee wasn't a cowgirl for nothing. She grabbed her lariat and gave chase.

Hart rushed down the aisle, tripping over a waste can, and fell to the floor. Doralee watched from the end of the aisle, twirling her lariat in the air above her. Hart looked up and saw what she was going to do, scrambled to his feet and began to flee again. But she let fly with the rope, and with a whoop and a holler, lassoed him around the shoulders.

He crashed to the floor and before he knew it, she was on top of him, grabbing his hands and feet and hog-tying him like a calf in the Cow Palace. "Yahoo!" she cried, and jumped up when she was finished, throwing her arms into the air like a champion cowgirl signaling the judges.

EPILOGUE

Doralee Rhodes, Sweetheart of Consolidated Ranch, sat back in her office chair with a can of beer in her hand, her feet in the common management *position, the white cowhide boots crossed on the blotter on the desk. She was enjoying the view. The sunset over the prairie was orange and streaked with red. She pushed her hat back on her head. Yes, this was going to be a peaceful night.*

She licked her lips. She could smell the coals, hear the sizzling. It was going to be a tasty barbecue. Tied on a spit, twirling slowly over the roasting embers, was none other than Frank Hart.

She'd tamed the varmint and fried his hide.

She smiled and crumbled the empty beer can with her fist.

And so ended another tale of the Old West.

"On a spit!" Judy bellowed, and then dropped the salami on a Ritz that she was eating. "God, suddenly I'm not so hungry anymore."

Violet was in stitches. "Hell, that story was only an appetizer. Serve up that chili, Doralee. That's just what he deserves, give him exactly what he gives us."

Doralee spooned out two bowls of chili. "Come on out on the porch, we'll have it out there. I'm hot from standing next to this damn stove."

"Roast Hart," Judy said, getting up. "Wouldn't give you seventy-nine cents a pound for that meat."

Violet giggled. "I can just see him, hanging there with that dumb look on his face, wondering what the hell happened."

They went outside and sat down on the old wicker furniture. *"Stud* cologne," Judy mused.

"Doralee, your story takes the cake. God, how I'd love to see it come to life."

"Come on Violet, I'll bet you can top it." Doralee put her feet up on the rocker. "Come on, how would you bump off the boss?"

"Hmm." Violet thought about it. She spooned some chili into her mouth and then closed her eyes. "Um, good. But I don't know. For me it would have to be a fairy tale. I love fairy tales."

"Hart in a fairy tale?" Judy asked.

"Yeah," Violet said. "Something horrible, gory, gruesome, but still kinda cute . . ."

Once upon a time, in a big glass and steel building in the heart of a major city, Franklin Hart, Junior, came out of his office and looked around for Doralee. Doralee was his secretary, and as often was the case, she was nowhere to be found. Frank Hart fumed. But he needed an important chore to be completed immediately, so he called on his next favorite flunky. "Violet," he shouted. "Coffee!" Then he went back inside his office and closed the door.

Violet, a very kind woman whose job requirements did not require that she make coffee for anyone but herself, looked up from her desk. "Yes, sir," she said softly, which was a surprise, for Franklin Hart calling to her for coffee usually perturbed her and made her stomach feel as though it were going to boil over. Not this time, however. This time Violet did not swear, she did not moan, she did not groan, nor kick anything, nor even throw him the bird, as was often the case. To the contrary, this time Violet flashed a smile of inner peace. You could almost hear strains of tranquil music over the typewriters in the background. Then Violet looked down at the pad on her desk.

On the pad, she'd drawn little cartoon animals, and now the animals had come to life. A fawn, beautiful and sleek in his brown, spotted coat, stood to the right of her, licking at her telephone unit. A plump possum was curled atop the typewriter. A trio of bushy-tailed rabbits jumped around the bottom of her swivel chair. And two animated bluebirds flew down from their nest in the light fixtures to sit on her shoulder as she got up from the desk and walked to the kitchen.

All the animals went with her, except one of the bunnies, who preferred to curl up and nap on the warmth of the seat of her chair.

In the kitchen, Violet performed a well-choreographed routine, almost dancing and singing to it, for she knew the rhythm of the actions so well. First the cup, la la la, then fill with coffee, la de dah! A little milk from the frig—the fawn snuck a lick as she poured it into the coffee—and two teaspoons of Skinny & Sweet from the cupboard.

The bluebirds sang sweetly, accompanying her as she stirred the brew, and a curious mousie poked his head around from behind the Bunn Coffee-Matic. Violet winked at him and then, very carefully, opened the top of her jeweled ring and poured some white powder into the coffee

Ominous, dark organ music filled the air.

The birds stopped singing happily.

The mouse cowered.

The rabbits perked their ears.

The fawn leaned close to Violet's body.

And the possum stood on his hind legs and hissed.

The coffee gurgled and bubbled and sent up a little mushroom cloud that scared the mouse right back into his hole. Violet assured all of her beautiful friends that it was all right, and then one of the bluebirds brought her a plastic spoon in its beak, and when Violet stirred the brew, the turbulence died down.

The animals breathed easier.

The music seemed brighter.

But the bottom of the spoon dissolved into the coffee.

Violet flashed a big smile and lifted the cup in front of her. Then, in procession, they all marched out of the kitchen and down the hall to Franklin Hart's office.

Violet entered without knocking. She left the door open behind her. "Your coffee, Mr. Hart," she sang.

He glanced up from his desk. "Oh, yeah. Put it down over here."

Violet cheerfully placed the cup of coffee alongside him. Preoccupied with the papers he was reading, he reached out and took the cup and drank a mouthful. Violet sat herself down on the corner of the desk with the bluebirds fluttering around her. Hart looked up, very surprised at this familiarity on her part. She smiled at him sweetly. "Some more coffee?"

"Coffee?" And then, suddenly, the low notes of a cello. Hart grabbed his throat and fell back in his chair. In front of all the eyes looking at him, he began to transform, Dr. Jekyll into Mr. Hyde, Count Dracula into the Vampire Bat, Puff the Magic Dragon into Godzilla. Smoke blew from his ears and his head spun around and around on his shoulders. Then he sprung from his chair, catapulting himself across the room, diving over the desk, somersaulting to the floor at Violet's feet.

Violet looked at him with nonchalant interest as she filed her nails.

The animals watched from the doorway—unlike Violet, they were all a bit frightened by the monster—as Hart crashed across the floor on all fours. He scurried and suddenly shot across the carpet again, only to complete another loop, like some kind of stunt pilot who'd forgotten his plane. He did it again and again and again. The animals were simply amazed.

But Violet grew bored. She'd finished her nails and put her file away. She gestured to the birdies to open the window. They fluttered over and pulled it up with their beaks. Violet moved to Hart's chair behind the desk. Hart himself, by this time, was bouncing up and down, ramrod straight, like a human pogo stick. He bounced higher and higher and higher, until there was a loud crash. Franklin's Hart's head was stuck in the ceiling lighting fixture.

Violet slowly shoved his chair over to where he was hanging by his skull, and then he dropped down into it. He looked at her. "I think there was something in that coffee."

"I think you're right." She matched his deadpan tone. Then she began to push him around the desk as if he were in a wheelchair.

"It was rat poison," he said.

"Right again," she said.

"You did it," he said.

"Right again." She smiled and stopped the chair in front of the open window. She looked out to be sure there was a lot of midday traffic on the street below.

"But why?" he asked.

"Why do you think?" was her reply

Violet went behind the chair and began to pump it up, higher and higher, until it reached the height of the window. Then she pulled a lever which tilted it back.

"Because I'm a sexist, egotistical, lying, hypocritical bigot?" he asked.

"Bingo," she said. And with that, she sweetly hit the lever, and the chair sprang forward, shooting F. Hart, Junior, out of the window.

EPILOGUE

Trumpeteers dressed in bright yellow and blue silk heralded the dawning of a new age.

Church bells pealed throughout the city.

Rainbows and showering rose petals surrounded a radiant Violet standing on the castle balcony, where she accepted the adulation of the cheering throng of Her Majesty's Office Workers.

Judy and Doralee, on either side of Violet, raised their golden goblets to the skies. Violet was handed a cup by the beautiful bluebirds, and the three women toasted to a time when all people would know an honest and happy day's work.

The bluebirds trailed ribbons through the cloud-filled sky.

The possum and fawn licked the spilled drops of wine.

The three rabbits curled up at Violet's feet.

Even the mouse peeked out from his hole and then ran free and scampered happily, knowing that forever more, even the thought of a "Hart" was banished throughout the land.

And they all lived happily ever after.

"I love the thought of him being catapulted out the window from his lousy chair," Doralee said. "He's always wanting me to fix that stupid thing, too cheap to get himself a new one."

Judy was giggling. "The coffee foaming over. Boy, what a delicious thought."

"Speaking of coffee," Violet added, "I think we could use some. I think I'm . . . how would Josh say it? I think I'm *coming down*."

Judy shook her head. "I wish this night never had to end. I can't remember when I had so much fun."

Doralee saw the car drive into the yard. "Dwayne's home! Listen, I want you to meet him. We can all have coffee together." They got up. "Listen, one thing I want to say, and I'm real serious now, this isn't any of that crazy fantasy stuff. I just want to tell you both how happy I am to have you as friends."

Judy smiled and put her arm around Doralee.

Violet winked.

Five

The next morning, Judy, Violet and Doralee got together on their coffee break. "God," Judy said, "it sure was fun. I went home, made my sandwich, put it in my purse, put my purse in the frig, and collapsed. I think I was still stoned."

"We'll have to do it again," Doralee said. "And Dwayne was happy to meet you both. He thought you were so very nice."

"He's not bad himself," Judy said.

"Speaking of sexy hunks of manhood," Violet said, "how's good old Hart this morning?"

"Hah!" Judy bellowed. "Haven't seen him at all today. Which is fine by me."

But Doralee had seen him. "He didn't say a word about yesterday, not a peep."

"That's strange," Violet said. "You'd think he'd apologize or something. The creep."

"He's too happy," Doralee explained.

"Happy?" Judy looked surprised.

"Yes. His wife left this morning for a two-month cruise in the South Seas."

"Lucky her," Judy muttered.

"I don't know," Violet said. "The poor thing still has to come back to him."

Doralee looked at the clock. "Oh, boy, Roz is probably ticking off the minutes. We'd better get back."

They picked up their things and deposited their coffee cups in the trash can.

"Let's have lunch today," Judy suggested.

"I can't," Violet explained. "I've got to go shopping. We're running out of cat food, fish food, ant spray and rat poison. I wish I could teach our cat to eat mice like cats are supposed to do, but I think she invites them in to play."

"Dick had a trap set in our attic once," Judy said. "One afternoon after 'General Hospital' was finished, I heard this scampering on the ceiling. Then a loud bang. I called him and told him and he said I should go up there and get the thing and toss it out."

Doralee shivered. "Did you?"

"You kidding? I let him do it. And it was so big and awful, even Dick had the willies when he tossed it out. Yuck."

"Yuck is right," Violet said. "I heard the same scampering this morning. The cat looked up, perked her ears, and purred. Crazy. So listen, I have to do that shopping. And don't look now, but dear Roz is giving us the evil eye from behind the third section."

And as on cue, Hart peered out of his door and, not seeing Doralee, shouted, *"Violet! Coffee!"* then withdrew into his office.

"I'm sorry, Violet," Doralee said. "I have to go to Hart's lawyer with some papers."

"That's OK," Violet groaned, "but please do me a favor and hurry back."

Violet got Hart his coffee, but there was no Skinny & Sweet left, so she substituted regular sugar. He sipped, then looked at her sharply. "Violet, that's sugar."

"Right."

"Don't you know sugar is bad for you?"

"Don't you know Skinny & Sweet is all chemicals, most of which have been found to cause untold diseases in laboratory animals?"

"I'm not a laboratory animal."

"Could have fooled me," she muttered.

"What?"

"Nothing, Mr. Hart."

"Well, listen, get another box of Skinny & Sweet while you're out at lunch."

"I'll be glad to—only because I'm going to the market anyhow."

She did her shopping, put the big bag of groceries in the kitchen, and returned to her desk. It was a hot day, the bag had been heavy and she had a headache on top of it all—she reminded herself to ask Josh if there was such a thing as a marijuana hangover. The moment she plopped into her chair, Hart's door opened. *"Violet! Coffee!"*

"Violet—coffee. Violet—coffee." She mimicked Hart. Just then Phoebe Hotz, a new girl who'd just been hired, came in with a problem about something she was working on, and Violet explained to her how to handle it. Five minutes later, Judy called to her, "Violet, Hart is shouting for you—he wants his coffee."

"God, I completely forgot." Violet picked up the cup and headed to the kitchen.

Betty Stokes was in the kitchen, cleaning up, a chore she never seemed to mind. It bothered Violet because she knew the reason Hart and Roz decided Betty was right for it was because she was black. Hart was already prejudiced if you were female; but a black female had *nothing* whatsoever going for her.

Violet was livid. "I swear, Betty, one of these days he's going to push me too far."

"More coffee?"

"Yup." Violet went to the machine and poured a cup.

"Maybe you should buy him a thermos. Oh, Violet, these things yours?"

"Yes, Betty, just leave it all there on the counter. I'll pack it up when I leave. I want to find a box in the copying room to cart them home; that bag isn't going to hold up." Violet went to the counter.

"We're out of Skinny & Sweet," Betty warned. "The boss is gonna blow a fuse."

"No, I got him some at lunch." Violet popped open the top of the Skinny & Sweet box and measured two teaspoonsful of the white powder into the coffee.

"Who the hell does he think he is, anyway? A miserable, petty, two-bit dictator, ordering me around like I'm some sort of flunky." She stirred the coffee so hard she nearly spilled it. "I get so mad at myself, I can't stand it."

"Look, he does it just to annoy you. Don't let him get to you. Besides, the day's almost over."

"You're right." Violet picked up the coffee. "I keep telling myself the same thing. But I can feel the pressure building inside me. I can't take much more of this, Betty, I really can't." She walked to the door, then turned back, calmer, serious. "Something, somewhere, sometime is going to snap. And then God help Franklin Hart, because I won't be responsible for my actions. But right now, I'm perfectly calm."

Betty smiled and went back to cleaning the lunch table.

Doralee came down the aisle just as Violet emerged from Hart's office. "How did it go?" Doralee asked.

"I'm calm, perfectly calm," Violet replied. She dropped her voice into the lower register and her eyes narrowed. "Actually, it's the sixth cup in the last three hours."

"Hang in there, honey," Doralee laughed. "It's almost five." She went to her desk and opened the folder she'd brought in with her. She could hear Hart shouting into the telephone. "No," he bellowed, "you listen to me! You'll get your money when I give it to you, understand that?" He paused, then yelled, "Good! And don't ever call me at this number again." He slammed down the receiver and threw himself back in his chair.

The faulty spring snapped again, tipping him over backward. His feet flipped up and hit the underside of his desk, the impact spilling the cup of coffee Violet had placed there. His head hit the credenza, and without a sound, he lapsed into unconsciousness.

Doralee, hearing the crash, leaped to her feet and rushed into Hart's office.

Bending over his inert body, she slapped his wrists and his face, trying to revive him. But there was no response.

Grabbing the phone, she hurriedly dialed the operator. "Get the paramedics, quick," she ordered. "Mr. Hart has collapsed in his office. Yes, sixteenth floor. Hurry!"

They hurried.

They were there within six minutes. Minutes later, they loaded him onto a stretcher and got him down to the waiting ambulance. Doralee grabbed her purse and jumped inside, peeking back through the little window at the still and silent figure of her boss, lying there on the stretcher, as the siren wailed and they zoomed across town.

Violet came off the elevator at 5:10 and found Judy waiting for her. "I'm sorry I'm so late," she apologized.

"Where have you been? You missed all the excitement."

"What happened?"

"They took Hart away in an ambulance."

Violet's eyes sprang wide. "No."

"He was unconscious. Had an attack or something. It happened so fast, nobody knew about it until they went in to get him."

"What about Doralee?"

"She went with him," Judy explained. She sounded concerned. "I hope it's not serious."

"Me too. Just some trifle that will keep him out of the office for the next twenty years."

Judy snickered. "Right. Listen, I just have to drop this off, and then we'll get going. I'll meet you at the elevator."

Violet nodded and went to the kitchen counter, where she had left the things she'd bought at lunch time. She grabbed the box of rat poison from the counter, just where she'd left it, and then realized she hadn't closed it tightly, and it—

Rat poison. Oh, my God in heaven. First she was confused. And then dumbfounded. Then she reached in the grocery bag and pulled out the tin of Skinny & Sweet. The two boxes matched perfectly, same size, same shape, same pry-up lid, same colors—except for the skull and crossbones on the rat poison.

Violet threw everything into the grocery bag, dashed out of the kitchen and ran to Hart's office, where a distraught Roz was cleaning up.

"Oh, Violet," Roz moaned, "isn't it awful about Mr. Hart?"

"How did it happen?" Violet asked, hoping to hear someone came in and shot him, strangled him, *anything,* before he had gotten to the coffee.

"He fell and hit his head on the window."

Violet took a deep breath, looked up, and thanked the Lord. But then she realized what probably *made* him fall and hit his head. "The coffee," she said.

"What?"

Panicked, Violet asked, "Where's the coffee cup?"

"Here." Roz picked it up. "It was by him on the floor. He must have been drinking it when he blacked out."

Violet held her breath and took back the "thank you" she had just uttered in her heart. She replaced it with, *How could you do this to me?* Then she asked Roz, "Quick, what hospital did they take him to?"

"Saint Ambrose," Roz answered.

Violet grabbed the cup, crushed it in her hand, and tossed the crumpled pieces into the waste can. Then she grabbed her grocery bag and ran out.

A sympathetic Roz moaned after her. "I know just how you feel."

"What's wrong?" Judy asked as she and Violet went down in the elevator.

Violet took a deep breath. "You know when I went to the market at lunch? I put the bag in the kitchen. I bought a box of Skinny & Sweet for Hart. I

made him five cups of coffee and put the Skinny &
Sweet in, just like always. But on the last cup I
goofed."

"What do you mean, goofed?"

"Betty was in there, talking to me, and I wasn't
paying any attention to what I was doing. Instead of
Skinny & Sweet I stirred rat poison into his coffee."

"My God." Judy was dumbstruck.

"I think I killed the bastard."

The doors opened on fifteen and they got out. "I
don't believe it!" Judy shouted. "How could you make
such a stupid mistake?"

"Shh," Violet said as they moved down the hall.

"You're right," Judy said, softer, "stay calm, we
have to stay calm. But, God, Violet, I don't understand
how it could have happened."

Violet pushed Judy into the corner of the time-
clock area, and pulled out the two boxes. "See these
tins? I thought this"—she held the one with the skull
and crossbones higher—"was the Skinny & Sweet.
They're almost identical, look—" She held it higher in
the air.

Judy grabbed it and shoved it into the bag. "My
God, someone could see you. Are you crazy? Punch
out. Where's your card?"

Violet pointed to her card, but her mind wasn't
on it. "I've got to tell them—"

Judy punched her out. "Tell who what?"

"The hospital, I've got to get there and tell them
what happened. They'll have to pump his stomach."

"Well, come on, then." Judy pulled Violet toward
the elevators to the parking garage. "We'll go together.
Just keep calm. Keep calm."

Violet started to shake. "Oh, my God, my God.
What if it's too late?"

"Don't get hysterical. Where's your car?"

Violet pointed. Then she bit her finger.

"Don't get hysterical!"

Violet took a deep breath as they ran for the **car**.
"You're right. You're right. Keep calm. Keep calm.

Think positive. He will not croak. I will get there and save him. Let's go!"

Judy jumped in and Violet got behind the wheel. "You sure you want to drive?" Judy asked. Violet started the car and backed it out, rubber burning, brakes screeching. She shot around the corner of the garage and careened through the little gate where she usually stopped to use her pass card. This time she took the gate with her. Violet definitely wanted to drive.

Judy hung on for dear life as Violet steered the car like someone possessed. "Watch out!" Violet screamed to a woman crossing the street, swerving just enough to miss her, but nearly giving the woman—and Judy—a heart attack. She gunned the engine and whipped around a corner, going due east, in the direction of the hospital. Then she saw a moving truck unloading furniture up ahead, blocking traffic for half a block, turned the car up a driveway and sped across seven front lawns, coming out on the other side of the truck. In her wake, Hurricane Violet left one mangled bicycle tire, two small trees, several flowers, and thirteen residents with their mouths open.

"We're going to make it, Violet," Judy said, encouragingly.

Violet screeched around a bus, into the wrong lane, and then made the final turn onto the street the hospital was on.

In the Emergency Room, Hart was placed on a trauma table. He opened his eyes, looked around, then sat up with a start. "What's going on?" he asked.

"You blacked out," the doctor said. "How do you feel?"

"I feel fine." Then he remembered. "I slipped off my chair and hit my head."

The doctor's hands were on that very head now, and he could feel where it happened. "You've got quite a bump up there. I think we'll take you upstairs to X ray."

Hart jumped off the table. "Just a minute, I don't need any X rays. My head's fine as it is."

"We should do some tests and make sure."

"You do the tests on yourself," Hart barked. "I know your racket and I'm not going to be suckered into paying hospital fees and doctors' bills for a little bump on the noggin."

Suddenly, the doors of the room burst open, and another gurney was wheeled in bearing an unconscious man about Hart's age.

"Cardiac arrest!" a medic shouted. "He's stopped breathing!" The doctor left Hart and hurried to the new arrival.

Hart watched for a moment as the doctors and nurses did everything they could to get the new man's heart going again; and then he simply opened the Emergency Room doors and walked out.

In the corridor, a plainclothes detective and a uniformed cop were talking. "He was our only witness," the detective said. "We had him all ready to testify. And now this."

"Don't give up hope yet," the policeman said.

Hart kept going. This hospital was not for him.

At the emergency doors, Violet spun the car around—it was still dragging the remains of a hedge she'd clipped off a yard down the block—and parked as close as she could to the entrance, in a *Doctors Only* space. Clutching the box of rat poison, she jumped from the car and rushed into the building, Judy hurrying behind her.

Doralee was standing at the admitting counter. "What are you two doing here?"

"Something terrible has happened," Judy whispered. "Violet put rat poison in Hart's coffee."

Doralee gasped.

"It was an accident. Look." Violet held up the box of poison. "Looks just like Skinny & Sweet."

"Where is he?" Judy asked. "We've got to speak to the doctor."

"They took him in the Emergency Room—there —behind those doors, the first one on the right."

"Oh, my God," Violet moaned, moving the box of poison behind her back. "There's a policeman. What's he doing?"

"I don't know," Doralee replied.

"The other one's a cop too," Violet whispered.

"How do you know?" Judy asked.

"Don't you ever watch TV?" Violet hissed. "They all dress like that."

"Kinda like Columbo?" Judy asked.

"Yeah."

The girls were slowly inching forward as the Emergency Room doors swung open and one of the medics who brought the gurney in came out to the hall. "Columbo" grabbed his arm and stopped him for a moment. "That guy they just brought in on the gurney," he said gruffly, "how is he?"

"Not so good," the medic said.

Violet and Judy turned to look at Doralee. Her face was sinking. She hadn't believed it ... until now.

"When can I speak to the doctor?" the detective asked.

"He knows you're here," the medic replied, and continued on down the hall.

"My God," Violet moaned, "they found out about it already. They got the *cops* already."

"Don't panic," Judy warned again, whispering in a commanding tone. "Just don't panic."

Just then the doctor emerged from the Emergency Room. The detective said, "How is he, doc?"

And the answer seemed to ring through the hall. "He's *dead*."

Violet, flattened up against the corridor wall, felt her stomach turn over.

"Can you tell what caused it?" the detective asked.

"Not without an autopsy," the doctor said.

Violet brought her hand to her heart. Well, thank God for that much. They wouldn't come after her right away. She could explain to her mother first.

But then the doctor continued. " . . . but I'm fairly certain it was some kind of poison."

Violet dropped her hand and felt her knees bending. She slid down the side of the wall in a faint, until Doralee and Judy grabbed her and held her up.

The doctor led the policeman and the detective past the three women. "Come down the hall to my office, we'll talk about it there." The men disappeared through a door, and then it closed without a sound.

Judy and Doralee helped Violet to the waiting area, sitting her down on a vinyl sofa. Violet's eyes were glazed over, her head feeling light, her heart heavy. She stared at Judy for a moment, then at Doralee. Then she said, "I killed him. My God, I really killed the bastard."

And then she fainted dead away.

Six

"It's all over, all over," Violet cried, as the girls tried to calm her. "Didn't you hear the doctor telling the cops he's going to do an autopsy? I may as well save them the trouble and give them the rat food right now."

Judy grabbed Violet's hands and slapped them. "No!"

But Violet lunged for Judy's purse and yanked the box of poison out of it. "Yes!"

"Give me that!" Judy said, trying to keep her voice down. She grabbed the box again and shoved it under her coat. "Someone will see it!"

"Who cares?" Violet retorted. "I'm finished. I'm a murderess. A killer. My poor kids."

"You're nothing until you're proven guilty."

"But they'll discover the poison when they do the autopsy," Doralee reasoned.

Violet suddenly wanted to live. "I'll get rid of the poison," she whispered.

"No, no," Judy said. "That won't help anything."

"Then I'll get rid of the body!"

Judy had heard enough. "Violet, this isn't *murder*. There were extenuating circumstances. It was an accident."

"An accident?" Doralee exclaimed. "But she was thinking about doing it just last night! And so were we."

"Yes," Judy admitted, "but she didn't do it on purpose."

"Maybe unconsciously I did do it on purpose." Violet shrugged dejectedly. "It's no use. I'm going to go to the pen."

Judy looked at Doralee. "We've got to get her a lawyer. Where's the phone?"

Dorales pointed across the room. "Over there."

"Got any change?"

"I think so." Doralee rummaged through her purse.

Judy turned to Violet and warned her, "You just sit right there, and don't, for God's sake, say anything to anyone."

"I'm going to lose my job!" Violet cried.

"Violet, shut up," Judy snapped, getting up.

Violet pounded her fist into the seat cushion. "I'm no fool. I killed the boss. You think they're going to let me keep my job after a thing like that?"

"Just sit still," Judy ordered. "We'll be right back."

Doralee and Judy went across the waiting room to the telephone alcove.

Suddenly, the doors to the Emergency Room banged open. Through them a medic wheeled out a gurney. On it was a white sheet. Under the sheet was a body.

"Mr. Hart . . . ?" Violet whispered.

Violet watched them push the gurney down the hall—until it was intercepted by the policeman. "Is this the guy for the autopsy?" the officer asked.

"Yeah." The medic nodded.

"Mr. Hart . . ." Violet whispered again, sure this time.

"The doctor wants to see you," the policeman told the medic. Leaving the gurney parked by the wall, both men went into the doctor's office.

Violet stared at the abandoned gurney with the sheet-covered figure. Poor Mr. Hart. He was so . . . alone. Yes, alone in this cold, sterile hall. They just . . . just left him there. Well, after all he wasn't going anyplace. . . .

Violet's eyes opened wide. What had she just said

to herself—he wasn't going anyplace? A crazy idea began forming in her head. Crazy, nuts, insane. But still, if it worked . . .

She inched her way over to the gurney and put her hands on the steel rail. She kicked the wheel lock—just as she'd seen the medic do—and all of a sudden she felt herself hurriedly pushing it down the hall. She had no idea where she was going. She just knew that some irresistible force was compelling her to get the evidence out of there. She came to the end of the corridor, saw the sign pointing to the main entrance of the hospital, and turned left, heading for it.

But up ahead of her, some doctors were holding a discussion. She reversed her direction, and turned the corner the other way. But that was a mistake as well, for coming down that hallway were three nurses and what looked like two more doctors. She thought fast, and instead of trying to run away again, she parked the gurney and opened the nearest door and walked into an office.

The doctors and nurses walked past the gurney without batting an eye.

Violet peeked out. All was clear. But as she was stepping out of the office, she noticed a white physician's coat hanging on a peg next to the door. She put it on without another thought, and then went back to the hall to fetch her corpse.

She pushed him toward the entrance again, until she saw a hospital security guard standing near the door. With her heart in her throat, she reversed her position and pushed the gurney back down the hall from whence it came.

Grimly determined to find an exit that wasn't guarded, Violet continued to the middle of the long hall. Ahead was the emergency area.

Just as she started on the last leg of her journey, a perky little Candy Striper came around the corner. "Excuse me," she said to Violet, "could you tell me where the coffee shop is, please?"

"What?"

"The coffee shop?"

Violet's heart skipped a beat. "Oh, the coffee shop. No. I'm . . ." She couldn't come up with anything but, "I'm new here." And then she added, "I don't drink coffee."

"I'm new here too," the girl said, smiling. Her nametag said *Buffie*. Violet thought she looked it. "Where do *you* work?" the girl asked.

"Um . . . downstairs," Violet replied, out of the blue.

"Oh." Buffie looked at her with awe. "In the morgue."

"That's right." Violet gestured to the body on the gurney.

"Then he's—" Buffie said.

"Yes, he's—" Violet said.

"How did he—" Buffie asked.

"Coffee—" Violet answered.

The girl blinked.

"Too much coffee. I'm just taking him outside for some air. I mean some fresh air for me. He's just coming along for the ride."

Buffie pressed her fingers over her lips. "Oops! You're a doctor."

"What?"

"I didn't notice your badge. Sorry."

Neither had I. Violet looked at the badge resting over her left breast. Sure enough, she was Dr. J. Modory. "I'm a doctor," Violet said, almost in surprise. Then she realized what was going on and snapped, "So why the hell am I talking to you? Piss off!"

Buffie, stunned, ran away as Violet turned the gurney and made a last, mad dash for the emergency doors at the end of the hall.

Doralee walked to the edge of the alcove just in time to see Violet, clad in her white doctor's coat, push the gurney out the emergency doors. She grabbed Judy. "Honey, Violet's flipped out!"

Violet pushed the gurney across the parking lot just the way she did with her shopping cart at the market. She stopped at the back of her car, opened the trunk and shoved the corpse, white sheet and all, into it.

Then she rounded the car and gave the gurney a shove, sending it careening across the parking lot, where it landed in a clump of bushes. She jumped in, started the car, shoved it into gear, and backed up— just as Judy and Doralee came running outside, looking for her.

"Come on," Violet yelled. "Get in! There's no time for talking."

Doralee opened the front door and she and Judy slid in alongside Violet. Judy could barely close the door before Violet hit the gas, speeding out of the parking lot and into the street, rounding the corner down the block, where she cut off the rest of the hedge she'd mowed down on her way in.

"Where are you going?" Judy asked. "Why are you driving so fast? I saw the point before, but now—"

"Look, I've got a great idea," Violet said. "They can't do an autopsy without a body."

"I *told you* I saw her pushing him!" Doralee screamed suddenly. *"She took the body!"*

"What's the big deal," Violet spit. "He's dead, isn't he?"

Doralee turned to Judy. "I told you she flipped! I told you!"

But Judy remained calm and collected. "Violet, where *is* the body?"

"In the trunk."

"In *this* car?!"

"Look," Violet sneered, "all we've got to do is get some cement blocks, chain them to his feet and pitch him off the end of the pier." She hung a fast left, just missing a motorcycle. "No one will ever know."

"You're crazy!" Doralee shouted. "They'll find it. They *always* find it."

"Violet, put your lights on," Judy said. "It's getting dark."

"Crazy am I?" Violet shouted back, at the same time pulling the switch for the lights, turning right, and heading for the waterfront. "Well, let me tell you something, Doralee Rhodes. They never found Jimmy Hoffa!" She stopped for a red light. But only for a moment, to check that there was no cross traffic. Then she hit the gas again, and the car charged forward.

Judy tried reason. "Violet, you've got to understand something. We're not criminals. It was an accident. You can't be blamed for anything. I was just calling a lawyer for advice."

"We're criminals now," Doralee interjected. "We've just stolen a corpse from a hospital. That sounds criminal to me."

"We can take it back," Judy said. "Yes, we'll just turn around and take it back."

Doralee shook her head. "No. We'll be caught if we go back now. They won't listen to us."

"Will you two stop arguing and think about where we can lay our hands on some cement," Violet shouted. Then she came to a wide boulevard, and suddenly turned onto it, passing cars left and right.

"What are we doing?" Judy shouted. They were going parallel to the waterfront.

"Slow down, Violet!" Doralee squealed, her hands firmly on the padded dashboard. "Slow down!"

"Wait, let's not panic," Judy said, "let's think things through."

"I'm going up to Old River Road. We'll sink him off the pier up there." Violet's voice almost had the ring of desperation rationalized.

"There's a restaurant up there," Judy said. "Let's pull in and stop for a while."

Doralee was horrified. "A *restaurant?* How can you think of food at a time like this? A restaurant! God Almighty!"

"I'm not hungry," Violet muttered.

"Our boss is as dead as a hammer in the back of this car," Doralee moaned, "and she wants to stop for dinner."

"I don't want to stop for *dinner!*" Judy explained. "I want to stop to *think.*"

Violet turned her head to look at the restaurant.

Doralee screamed, "Keep your eyes on the road! You're driving like crazy!"

"So? I thought you said I *was* crazy?"

"You *are* crazy!" Doralee howled. "You're driving like a madman!"

"Wrong," Violet corrected. "I'm a mad*woman!*"

"LOOK OUT!" Doralee screamed. A garbage truck was crossing the road. The light was red.

Violet spun the wheel to avoid crashing into the truck. The car went into a spin, twisting around twice before it slammed up sideways against a trash dumpster in a deserted lot.

There was a long silence, and finally, they all opened their eyes. They were shaken, but not hurt.

Violet looked in the rearview mirror. "It was nothing. We'll be out of here in a—" She stepped on the gas but the car didn't move.

Violet put her head out the window. "The front fender. It's hitting the tire."

She hit the gas and got the car off the sidewalk. It landed in the street with a bump. They all got out and looked at it.

In the dim streetlight, Doralee examined the fender. "It's not so bad. We just have to pull the metal back." She bent forward and pulled on the crinkled side of the car above the tire. "We need a crowbar or something," Doralee decided, and walked around the back to find the rear left light blinking. "Judy, turn the blinkers off."

Judy reached inside the car and clicked them off.

Then Doralee opened the trunk, took a deep breath, and looked at the sheet-covered body. The tire iron had to be near the spare, but that's where Hart's head was. . . . Oh, hell, she'd seen him alive enough times, why would it be any different looking at him dead? She pushed the sheet away to search for the tire iron and it uncovered the head of the corpse. She froze.

She stood there for a moment, looking up to the sky, with her eyes shut. It was as if she was clearing her head, shaking off the hallucination. Then she looked back again. And she was sure this time. "Er . . . Judy. Would you come back here for a second."

Judy wondered why the change in Doralee's voice. She walked around the side of the car. "What?"

"Look."

Judy looked. Her hand went over her mouth. "Who's that?"

"I don't know."

"Where's Hart?"

"I don't know."

"Oh, my God." Judy put her hand on her cheek and shook her head. "Did she . . . ?" She bit her thumb. "Oh, my God."

"Um, Violet," Doralee sang, "would *you* come back here for a second?"

"What's the matter with you two?" Violet said as she joined them. "We've got to get—" She stopped cold, looking down into the trunk. "Who's that?"

"I don't know," Doralee answered.

"I've never seen him before, either," Judy added.

"What do you mean, you don't know?" Violet said, shocked. "What happened to Hart's body?"

"It's not here," Doralee explained, as if talking to a child. "What do you think, it got up and walked away?"

Violet shrugged. "I guess I must have made a mistake."

Doralee exploded. "You steal the wrong body from the hospital, and all you can say is you made a mistake?"

"It could happen to anyone."

"Oh, this is awful," Judy moaned. "It's so improper. So disrespectful."

"He's dead," Violet reminded her; "he doesn't mind. Look, there's nothing to get excited about. We'll take it back."

"What?" Doralee exclaimed.

"No harm's done," Violet replied. "Come on. We'll just turn around and take it back."

Doralee put her hands on her hips and faced

Violet in the streetlight. "Oh, sure. That's great. We waltz in there and tell them we're sorry, an honest mistake. Maybe they'll give us Hart's body in exchange."

"There's no need to get sarcastic," Violet snapped.

Doralee screamed at the top of her lungs. *"You took it, you take it back!"*

Judy stomped her foot. "No, no. Stop it!" They quieted down. "Look, we're all in this together. We must stay calm." Violet was sick of hearing that word already. "Let's just fix the fender and drive back to the hospital. We'll figure out a plan to drop off the body and then we'll all sit down and decide what to do next."

There wasn't another word.

They found the tire iron, pried the fender from the tire, and closed the trunk. Then they piled in the car again. Violet made a wide U-turn, and went back the way they had come. "I really didn't want to go out Old River Road at night anyhow," Violet said. "Place gives me the creeps."

They drove for a few minutes—sanely, this time —and each one of them tried to come up with a way to deposit the man in the trunk back on his gurney in the hospital corridor. Doralee suggested Violet putting on Judy's glasses, wrapping a scarf around her head, running in with the dead man, acting hysterical until the emergency room staff came to grab him, and then running out to the getaway car. But Violet said it wasn't safe enough, the disguise might not work, and did Doralee realize what a dead man weighed?

Violet voted for simply dumping the body on the front lawn. Someone would see it sooner or later, one of the good nuns who ran the place, or a doctor, or a visitor. But it was voted down as too risky.

Then Judy suggested one of them go in and get a wheelchair. They could put the body into it, set him in place, and Violet would wheel him into the hospital and park him someplace.

"Why me?" Violet asked.

"Because *you* took him!" Doralee yelled.

"Yes, that," Judy said, "but mainly because you're the one dressed like a doctor."

Violet realized she was still in the white coat. "Oh."

"Yes, Doctor J. Modory," Doralee said, reading the badge as she reached over Judy to see it. "What's the 'J' stand for, *jerk?*"

"Julia," Violet replied. Then added. "You know, it's not a bad plan. It might work if we can find a wheelchair."

"I saw a couple by the emergency entrance when we were there," Doralee recollected. "I think it's a good idea."

Judy shook her head and then rested it on the seat back. "I just wish we knew what happened to Hart."

Doralee folded her arms in resignation. "We'll find out soon enough." Her ears perked. "What's that?"

Judy heard it too. A siren. She turned and saw the flashing red light. "It's a motorcycle cop," she said.

Violet gritted her teeth, gripping the wheel so hard her fingers hurt. "What do I do? Make a break for it?"

Doralee reached into her purse. "I don't know— I've got my gun!"

"PUT THAT AWAY!" Judy screamed. Then she took a deep breath. "Let's not panic. Stay calm."

"Okay, pull over," Doralee said, still holding onto her pistol in her purse. "But be ready for anything."

"But what if he—"

The siren sounded even louder.

"For Chrissakes," Judy yelled, "pull over!"

Violet hit the brakes and stopped at the side of the road.

The cop parked his motorcycle and walked over to Violet's window. He leaned down to speak to her. "Good evening, ladies. May I see your license and registration, please?" he asked Violet.

"Why? I wasn't speeding."

"I didn't say you were. Your taillight is blinking."

Their hearts skipped a beat. "It is?" Violet said.

"Are your signals on?" he asked her.

She checked. "No."

"Then it must be a short in the trunk."

"A short in the trunk?" She smiled at him then turned her head to the others. "We've got a short in the trunk."

"He means a *stiff* in the trunk," Doralee whispered.

Judy elbowed her.

"It's probably only a defective wire or something," the cop explained. "You want to take a look?"

Violet turned to Judy. She swallowed hard. "Do we want to take a look?"

"No," Doralee cried out, leaning over Judy to look up at him. "We can't, officer. We have no time. We're on an . . . emergency."

Judy picked up on it. "Yes. That's right." She pointed to Violet. "She's a doctor."

"You're a doctor?" the cop said to Violet.

"What do you think I am, a beautician?" she snapped, turning her name tag for him to see.

"I'm sorry, Doctor Modory," he said, apologetic. "I didn't see your badge. What's the trouble?"

"The trouble is I'm taking this woman to the hospital. She's very sick."

"Which one of you is sick?" he asked, putting his head half-way through the window.

"I am," Doralee said.

"I am," Judy said.

They looked at each other, then tried again.

"She is," Doralee said.

"She is," Judy said.

Violet kicked Judy's leg. "They're *both* sick."

"Oh," he rubbed his head. Then he noticed something in Judy's lap, and when she saw him looking at it, she tried to cover it with her coat. "What's that you're hiding?"

"Hiding?" Judy said, smiling.

"Yes. Under your coat."

"This?" She lifted the box.

"Yes."

"It's rat poison."

"She ate it," Violet remarked.

"What?" The cop blinked.

"She *ate* the *rat poison*," Violet said again, as if talking to a wall. "That's *why* they're sick."

The cop was astonished. "You ate rat poison?"

Doralee chimed in, "I thought it was Skinny & Sweet." She grabbed her stomach and let out a long, low moan.

"It looks *exactly* like Skinny & Sweet," Judy explained. "Except that it has a little skull and cross-bones on the label."

Doralee kept it up, sounding more like she was in labor than poisoned. "Can't we go now, please? I'm not feeling very well."

Violet was suddenly perturbed. "My God, did you hear that? She's not feeling very well. I've got a dying woman on my hands and you want to look for a short in the trunk?"

The cop looked nervous. "I'm sorry, doctor."

"If we don't make it to the hospital," Violet shouted, "I'm holding you responsible."

Doralee moaned, "Oh, please, Julia, I'm not going to make it."

Violet turned. "Julia?"

"*Doctor* Julia," Judy reminded her.

"Oh, yes, well," Violet said, remembering her name. Then she yelled at the cop again, "You may have the death of this woman on your hands if you detain us any longer."

"Don't worry," he said, putting on his gloves, "I'll give you an escort."

"An escort?" Violet asked, hoping she heard wrong.

"Good Lord," Doralee muttered.

"He's going to give us an escort," Violet said, calmly, but her eyes filled with horror.

"Oh, my God." Judy bit her thumb.

"Hang on, ladies," the cop said, buckling the strap under his helmet. "Just follow me." He started back toward his bike.

But Violet gunned the engine, and shoved the car in gear. "Forget it, buster," she called to him. "We can't wait." And she hit the gas and left him standing on the roadside, in a cloud of dust.

"What's he doing?" Judy asked.

Doralee was hanging her head out the window. "He's just standing there. Staring at us."

"The nerve of that guy," Violet muttered. "Stopping a doctor in an emergency."

"But you're not a doctor," Doralee reminded her.

"*He* doesn't know that!" And Violet hit the gas, spinning around a corner, heading back toward Saint Ambrose.

Violet killed the lights down the block from the hospital and slowed the car.

"The wheelchairs are by the doors," Doralee said. "You need to back in a space where we can get him into a chair and wheel him in."

"Good God," Violet muttered, turning into the emergency entrance. "The lights are too bright there. We have to park in the dark."

"Yes," Judy said, "Violet's right. We can wheel him across the parking lot. We can't take the chance of someone coming out and seeing us loading him into a wheelchair."

Violet steered across the parking lot, into a dark section near some bushes. "Look," she said, pointing. "That's the thing I wheeled him out on." The gurney still lay half on it's side in the green shrubs; no one had yet discovered it. "Could mean they still don't know he's gone."

"Our lucky night," Judy said, sarcastically.

"Well, you have to look on the bright side." Violet turned the car off "You two have him ready when I come back with the chair." She handed Judy the key and got out of the car.

"Anything you say, Doc," Judy answered as she and Doralee went around to the trunk.

Several minutes later, Violet came pushing a wheelchair across the parking lot, but she was obviously having a difficult time. The front left wheel was rubbing against the frame, forcing her into pushing the chair in a zigzag pattern. "I would pick a wheelchair that needs a wheelchair," she grunted when she reached the girls.

Judy had the trunk open, and Doralee was already yanking at the body's feet. Violet positioned the chair. Then they all pulled together.

"I feel like a grave robber," Judy said. "Violet, grab an arm, it's going backwards—"

"Oh, damn." Violet lost her balance, which in turn caused Doralee to slip, and the body slid into a position half in and half outside of the trunk.

"Come on, come on," Judy directed, "all we have to do is grab the top half and turn him around and put him in the chair."

"He must weigh about three hundred pounds," Doralee muttered, grabbing him under the arm. "Oh, Lord, his wife probably poisoned him because he refused to wear deodorant."

"Have some respect for the dead," Violet whispered, and heaved. They got him up straight, turned him around, and then plopped him into the wheelchair. But the chair rolled away under the weight, letting the body slip down onto the pavement.

"You didn't brake the wheels!" Judy hissed at Violet.

"I could barely get it across the lot," Violet explained, annoyed. "How am I supposed to know it's going to move backwards easier than it goes forward?"

The girls regrouped and again lifted the body into the chair. This time the body slumped forward, and if it hadn't been for Judy's quick thinking—lifting her knee—it would have toppled face-first to the pavement.

"We've gotta strap him up," Doralee said.

"With what?" Judy asked.

Violet had an idea. "I know, I know, Josh gave me this——" She rummaged in the trunk and pulled out what looked like a fuzzy, green, deflated bicycle tire. "He won it at a carnival."

"What is it?" Judy asked.

"One of those furry steering-wheel covers. He won some dice to go with it, but his girlfriend took them."

"How are we going to tie him in with that?" Doralee asked.

"Just slip it over his head. . . ." Violet proceeded to pull the green elastic band over the head, down to the chest and around the back of the chair. It worked perfectly.

Still, something didn't look right. "He's not natural," Doralee said.

"Of course not," Violet whispered, "he's dead."

"I mean the arms. You have to put the elastic under his arms so they can stay on the arm rests."

"She's right," Judy agreed, and they pulled the man's arms up from under the green band, and then arranged them on the sides of the chair. Violet grabbed the sheet from the trunk and covered him, tucking it in at his sides.

"He still looks dead," Doralee said.

"Of course he does," Judy snapped. "But it's the best we can do. You think were gonna get him to do a song and dance for his arrival?"

"I've got it!" Violet went into the backseat. Sure enough, there was the sun hat she'd tossed back there the day she was working on the garden and remembered to run to the store before it closed. "Stick this on his head."

Doralee pushed the floppy-brimmed hat over the man's head. She giggled. "He looks drunk."

"Great," Violet said, getting in position at the handles of the chair, "that's a lot better than dead."

"Ready?" Judy asked.

Violet nodded. "Now remember, you two divert

the attention of anyone in there—I don't care if you have to batter each other with your purses—just get them looking away from me."

Doralee said, "With that white coat, no one will think to question it. Come on, Judy."

Judy followed Doralee.

And Violet brought up the rear, straining to push the broken chair. Finally, they reached the smooth surface of the hospital portico.

"Go to it, ladies," Violet said.

"Right, Doc," Judy answered as she and Doralee entered the emergency area.

While they inquired as to a Mr. Franklin Hart, explaining they were secretaries of his who were concerned, Doctor Julia Modory wheeled in a patient and continued down the hall.

Five minutes later, Violet, no longer in her white coat, sat waiting in the car as Judy and Doralee hurried across the parking lot. They jumped in. "How did it go?" Violet asked.

"Nobody batted an eye," Judy said.

"How was it on your end?" Doralee asked, breathless, shutting the car door.

Violet circled her thumb and forefinger and gave them a thoroughly assured look. "Piece of cake."

"Thank God that's over," Doralee sighed, putting her head back. "We can relax."

"Not quite," Violet reminded her. "What about Hart?"

"We couldn't find out anything about him," Doralee explained. "They either don't know or won't tell us."

"Well," Violet asked, "what do we do?"

"Nothing." Judy said it decisively. "We wait till they come to us. Just go to the office in the morning and pretend that nothing has happened."

Violet started the car and backed out of the space. She turned on the lights this time and headed out of the lot, waving a little good-bye to the hospital. "I'll tell you one thing," she said softly, "if this day's been an example of what marijuana leads to, I never want to see another joint for the rest of my life."

Inside the hospital, two cleaning ladies were mopping an empty hallway. One of them opened the door marked *TOILET* and went inside, propping the door open with the pail of water and Lysol. She clicked on the light and immediately noticed the white doctor's coat tossed in the sink. "Now, why'd somebody do that?" the woman muttered, going to pick the coat out of the basin. "Doctors gettin' so they're sloppier than the visitors." She grabbed the coat and took it outside to the hamper down the hall.

The other cleaning lady entered the bathroom and stood leaning with her mop under her chin. In the stall was a man sitting in a wheelchair, wrapped in a white sheet, a wide-brimmed hat on his head. The woman lowered her head a little and stared, then moved forward and lifted the hat. The head fell forward. "Vera," the cleaning woman called out to her friend, "we've got another stiff in the john."

Seven

The executive elevator doors opened. Franklin Hart stepped out, flashing his customary phony smile, and walked down the corridor to his office. Judy, coming out of the copying room just as he passed, barely squeaked, "Good morning, Mr. Hart," as the papers she was holding slid to the floor.

Hart took no notice. Near his office, he bumped smack into Violet. She jumped back, startled. Her face went white. "Jesus, Violet, you look like you've just seen a ghost," Hart remarked. He left her rooted to the spot, speechless.

Hart strode past Doralee. "Doralee," he threw over his shoulder, "no calls at all. I don't want to be disturbed for any reason."

Doralee gulped and barely nodded as he disappeared into his office. Then she looked up and saw Violet. And Violet turned and saw Judy. And Judy mouthed, *"Meet me in the can."*

A few minutes later, they convened in the ladies' room. "All the running around last night was useless," Doralee said.

Violet sat on the vanity and shrugged. "Damn."

Doralee continued. "He must have left the hospital with just a little bump on his skull."

"But I tell you," Violet said, "I did put the poison in his coffee."

"But he obviously didn't drink it," Judy pointed out.

Doralee shook her head. "I don't know how we

could have been so stupid." Suddenly, she stiffened. "Did anyone check under the stalls?"

Violet nodded. "Yes. No one's here."

Judy splashed cold water on her face. "Well, I propose we forget about the whole thing." She found she was dripping on the glasses hanging on the chain around her neck. "It never happened."

"That's okay by me," Violet said. "Cops. Corpses. I'll never mention it again." She thought about it. "My God, stealing a body from a hospital, running away from the police, having the guts to go and put it back—who would believe a word of it anyhow?"

Judy dabbed toweling on her face. "It is amazing, isn't it?"

"Thank God it's Friday," Doralee said, smiling finally. "Let's all start the weekend with a drink at Charlie's after work. What do you say?"

"Count me in," Judy answered.

"I could use one right now," Violet said.

"Well," Judy said, "maybe we could get Margaret to pass the bottle."

"I'll leave well enough alone," Violet said. "God was with us last night. I don't want to push my luck. We'd get canned and potted at the same time."

Judy felt better. "You know, we've been real lucky. I'm just glad this whole mess is finally over."

"Right, honey," Doralee said. "And we'd better get back before the warden realizes we're gone."

"See you later," Violet said.

Judy pushed her glasses up on her nose and followed them out of the room.

A few moments after they left, one of the stalls doors began to open slowly. Sitting cross-legged on the john, the last of her notes scribbled on the wad of toilet paper in her lap, Roz the Warden smiled sweetly to herself and put her pen back into her tweed jacket.

"Is this accurate?" Hart asked.

Roz stood at attention before his desk. "Yes, sir."

"Come on."

"It is no joke, sir."

"They actually *said* all this?" He was incredulous.

"Yes, sir. As clearly as I could make out. My notes were a little . . . um, fuzzy."

He was reading a typed transcription of her Charmin steno pad. He shook his head and tossed it on his desk. "Quite a story. No wonder they looked shocked to see me today. Stealing corpses, eluding the police. Maybe they knew you were hiding and just wanted to pull your leg."

She sneered. "I don't think so. In any event, I believe you should be aware of that coffee business."

He chuckled to himself. "Yes, I think I could use that to some advantage." He seemed lost in thought for a moment, and then looked up at her. "Thank you, Roz. You do a great job around here. In fact," he stood up, holding out his hand, "I always think of you as 'one of the guys.' "

She shook his hand, beaming. "Thank you, Mr. Hart!" She took a step back, obviously elated, standing at attention. "That's what I strive for!" Then she gave him a little salute, and marched out of his office.

The clock hit five and the typewriters ceased in mid-clack. Doralee put on her coat and grabbed her purse. "Judy, wait for me," she called, "I'll just be a second." Then she hurried into Hart's office.

"Yes?" Hart said, deep into something at his desk.

"It's five o'clock, Mr. Hart," she reminded him. "You wanted to see me."

"Doralee, I'd like you to come up to the house tonight."

"Wait a minute, Mr. Hart. I'm not working tonight. It's Friday, remember?"

"Who said anything about *working?*" He stood and walked over to her. "By the way, Doralee, have you ever heard of strychnine?"

She was puzzled. "I think it's a poison."

"That's right." He walked around. "I was just on

the phone with the hospital. They found traces of it in the tests they ran after pumping my stomach yesterday."

Her stomach felt like it needed pumping suddenly. "What? But you told me that you had just hit your head."

"I had to be sure. You need that kind of evidence when you accuse someone of murder."

"Mu . . . murder?" she squeaked.

"Yeah." He stopped walking and faced her. "You and Violet and that girl, Judy, tried to murder me yesterday by putting rat poison in my coffee."

"Oh, my goodness," she said. She was shaking.

"That's good," he snarled, watching her cringe. "You should be scared. I know all about it. All I have to do now is pick up that phone and tell the police."

She looked at the phone, and then suddenly turned to him, grabbing his arm, pleading. "But, Mr. Hart, it was a mistake! Violet put the rat poison in by accident."

He pulled away. "Maybe a jury would believe her and maybe they wouldn't. The question is, do you want to take that chance?"

Now she pulled away. "What are you driving at?"

"You could make me forget all about it if you come up to my house tonight."

For a moment, she wished Violet's coffee had worked. "Mr. Hart, you are *disgusting.*"

"Is that a 'no'?" he asked. Then, with dramatic gesture, he picked up the receiver and began to dial the phone.

Doralee tossed her coat on the desk. She rushed to him and pushed the button on the cradle of the phone. "Mr. Hart, I beg you. Think of what you're doing. I have a husband, Violet has a family. Why would you want to ruin our lives?"

He stopped her hand and started to dial again. "I'm not the one who started this," he said matter-of-factly. "It was you three who did all the plotting . . . and now you gotta pay the consequences."

She grabbed the extra phone unit and tossed it to the floor. "I won't let you do this!" she shouted.

But he was undaunted. "There's another phone over here," he said, gesturing to the extension sitting on the table next to the sofa. "In fact, here's something else I'd like you to hink about." He opened the small box on the table and picked up her scarf. "I get very upset when my presents are returned." He waved it in the air.

She stomped her feet. "You are rotten, Mr. Hart! I never thought I'd say this about another human being, but you are *evil!*"

He sat back on the sofa and nodded, smiling his approval. "I love it when you're angry." Then he reached out and picked up the receiver.

"I swear, Mr. Hart," Doralee warned with venom in her tone, "if you touch that dial, I'll rip it out of the wall."

He laughed and stuck his finger in the dial.

Doralee leaped from where she stood, grabbed him as if roping a steer, and they fell from the couch to the floor, where she wrestled him into a half nelson.

"Doralee!" he gasped. "My God, you're strong. Don't tickle me, now. . . ."

She didn't tickle him. She socked him in the ribs, and jumped up and off him and grabbed the telephone and ripped the extension cord right out of the wall. Then, using the line as a rope, she hog-tied him, binding his hands and feet. Yahoo! She jumped up.

"Doralee, what have you done here? What's the meaning of this? Get me loose."

"Don't move," she ordered.

"Goddamn it, I feel like a fool. Let me go or I'm really going to lose my temper."

"Don't say *anything*," she warned.

"Do you want me to yell for help? Goddammit, Doralee, if you don't untie me this minute, I'll—"

She grabbed the scarf he'd given her. "Thanks for the nice present, boss. Now, eat it." She balled it up and stuffed it in his mouth.

Doralee took ten deep breaths to get herself under

control, and then opened the office door and slipped out to find Roz waiting for her right outside.

"Is Mr. Hart still here?" Roz asked.

"Yes, but he's tied up at the moment."

Roz shrugged. "Oh, well, I guess it can wait until Monday."

Doralee smiled. "Have a good weekend, Roz. See you on Monday, then."

"Don't count on it," Roz muttered, and huffed off.

Doralee stuck out her tongue. "Snitch." Then she hurried over to Violet's desk.

Judy was waiting there for her. "Ready?"

"No. Something awful has just happened. Where's Violet?"

"She's in the storage room. What's the matter?"

"Hart knows everything about last night."

"My God, how?"

"The fat ass with the bun."

"She *was* in a stall!"

Doralee wrung her hands together. "He believes we were trying to murder him. He was going to call the police and have us arrested."

"Dear Lord!"

"Go inside and keep an eye on him. I've got to get Violet."

"Keep an eye on him? He'll—"

"No he won't. I tied him up."

"You what?"

"Tied him up. You'll see. Just lock the door and don't let anyone in. I'll get Violet. She'll know what to do."

Judy opened Hart's door and her mouth fell open. "Oh, my Lord God in Heaven," she moaned, not believing her eyes. She closed the door and remembered to lock it. "Mr. Hart, I'm truly sorry."

He thrashed around on the rug, moaning and gurgling.

"What?" she asked. "I can't understand what you're trying to say." She knelt beside him and pulled the scarf from his mouth.

"Thank God one of you has come to your senses," Hart said to her. "Now, let me loose."

"Mr. Hart," Judy explained, "I'm sure Doralee didn't mean any harm. She just wanted to explain what happened—what *really* happened last night."

"Untie me."

She didn't move.

"Please."

"I . . . I can't."

"What?"

"I can't do that until they come back."

"Do you think I'm going to run away? I give you my word of honor that I won't do anything if you just get me loose."

Judy looked at him hesitantly.

"Um, Judy," he grimaced, "there's an element of *pain* involved here . . ."

"I'm sorry," she said. "I'll loosen them a little." She began to untie the telephone cord. "You see, Mr. Hart, all that happened last night was a series of misunderstandings. Violet didn't try to kill you. She just *accidentally* put the poison in your coffee." She got a knot opened and then pulled part of the cord through the other at his feet. "The poison was really meant to go to another rat—I mean, to the rat at Violet's house, a mouse kind of rat I mean. The poison looked just like—"

Hart suddenly kicked out, scrambled free, and shoved Judy aside. "Get out of the way!"

She rolled across the floor as he lunged for the phone. "But, Mr. Hart, you gave me your word!"

"I lied!" He banged his fingers down on the cradle and then turned the dial with little success. "The phone's dead." He slammed it down.

"Mr. Hart," Judy said, on her knees, "you're not leaving this office."

"Just watch me!" He went around the desk, and she got up to her feet just in time to have him shove her backward into the chair at the side of the desk. She landed on something hard.

Hart was heading for the door. "This thing has

gotten out of hand. No one is going to make a fool out of me in my own office. I'm calling the police." He turned the handle and opened the door.

Judy reached under her and pulled out Doralee's purse. Thinking fast, she reached into it. "Hold it right there," she warned.

Hart turned back and froze. Judy was pointing a .38 pistol right at his nose. "My God," he said in a shocked monotone, "you're as crazy as they are."

"Close that door or I'll shoot."

He ducked and ran out the door and slammed it shut as the gun fired.

The glass in the door exploded in a burst. Hart stopped in his tracks and raised his hands in the air, shouting, *"Don't shoot! Don't shoot!"*

Violet and Doralee arrived running as Judy stepped through the broken glass of the door and lowered the pistol.

Violet, white-face and trembling, moved forward. "What are you *doing?*"

"He was going to call the police." Judy waved the gun at Hart who was still standing with his hands up.

"Oh God." Violet sat down at Doralee's desk. "Oh, God."

"Oh God is right," Doralee moaned. "Now what are we gonna do?"

Judy pointed the gun in Hart's direction. "We don't have much choice," she said, as Hart, near tears, cringed.

"I guess not," Doralee said with resignation.

Violet looked at her boss. "Okay, you. Back into the office. We've got work to do."

Hart moved slowly, as Judy walked backward through the broken glass, keeping him covered with the gun. The others followed in procession.

Violet's car left the parking garage and eased into the sparse night traffic of the downtown area. They sat as they had the night before, Violet driving, Judy in the middle, Doralee on the passenger side. No one said a word for several minutes. It was uncanny. It was happening again. Only this time they were certain the guy in the trunk was Franklin Hart.

Judy finally spoke. "I just feel so terrible doing this to him."

"We got him past the security guard, didn't we?" Violet said.

"Yes, but . . ." Judy didn't know what to say.

Doralee did. "Look, we'll get him up to his place and try to reason with him. It's so far back from the road that if he starts hollering, no one will hear."

"You really think he'll understand?" Judy asked.

Violet turned onto the boulevard which led to the suburb where Hart lived. "Has he got a choice?"

The streets were quiet, the moon full. Hart's street was dark, the cul-de-sac deserted. Violet steered the car past manicured bushes, aiming for the house which loomed silently in the distance.

"My God," Judy said, "takes two weeks to get up the driveway."

"Here we are, Franklin," Violet sang over her shoulder, "home to Mandalay at last." She felt a tinge of revenge in delivering her boss to his expensive Tudor-style castle in the trunk of her beat-up Pontiac. She turned around in the circular drive, then backed the car up to the house and shut off the engine. "All set?" she asked the others.

"Seems like we've done this scene before," Doralee groaned, getting out of the car. She went around and opened the trunk. "Hi," she said to the bound and gagged figure.

He kicked his feet against the spare.

Guilt was already beginning to eat at Judy. "There's got to be a way we can make him understand."

"Worry about that later," Violet said, reaching in to grab Hart's legs. "Right now we have to get him inside."

Doralee took an arm. "Heave ho."

Hart was on his feet.

"Okay, buster," Violet snapped, "hop."

Hart didn't move.

Violet was mad. "What do you think we're gonna do, carry you? *Hop.*"

Hart still refused to move.

"Doralee," Violet commanded, "get your gun."

Hart hopped.

With a little urging Hart managed to hop right up the staircase and into his bedroom. Judy took the gag from Hart's mouth as Doralee sat on the bed holding the gun. Violet ordered him into the chair at his wife's dressing table, and then Doralee gave Judy the gun and bound his feet to the legs with rodeo-type knots. "If he gets outta here, he's gonna have to take that chair with him," she said, looking at her handiwork.

And then all three tried to reason with him. But it was no use.

"You'll pay for this!" he kept repeating. "I swear you'll pay for this! I'll see you in prison before I'm through—"

Violet couldn't stand it anymore. She grabbed a sock from his bureau and stuffed it in his mouth. "Now, with you quiet for a while, your ears can do all the work. Listen, because we're going to explain it all one more time. . . ."

And they did.

Then they pulled the sock out, hoping this time he'd be calm and admit he understood what a silly mistake it had all been.

But he went berserk. *"Kidnapping!"* he yelled. "Kidnapping and attempted murder—roped, beaten, poisoned, made to be a fool—"

"What are you talking about?" Doralee shouted back. "Who made you out to be a fool?"

"You made me *hop!*" He drew in a breath and shuddered. "That was disgusting." Then he started ranting again. "I won't rest till you all get twenty years, you hear me? *Twenty years!*"

Finally, the three women walked out. Doralee

shut the bedroom door and leaned against the bannis-
ter. "Does this mean we've lost our jobs?"

Judy gave her a rueful look, and continued down
the steps.

Violet shrugged and followed.

And so did Doralee.

"I'm hungry," Judy said.

Violet moaned. "God, yes. We haven't eaten anything since lunch."

Doralee groaned. "I didn't even *have* lunch."

"Let's see what he's got in the old ice box," Judy
said, making her way through the dining room to the
kitchen. She looked up at the chandelier. It sparkled
gold and the sconces glittered with the lights. "Not bad
on his salary."

"Yeah," Violet sneered, "on the money *we* de-
serve." She looked up. "That thing should only drop
on his head."

"Come on, Violet," Doralee said, "maybe he's got
some caviar and champagne in there. . . ."

"Lousy chicken salad," Violet said, munching a
sandwich.

"And not a regular soda in the place," Doralee
added, drinking milk. "All diet junk."

"With his passion for Skinny & Sweet, did you
think you'd find anything else?" Violet said.

"Don't mention that stuff," Judy said as she
licked the peanut butter from her finger. "We *have* to
do something. We can't keep him up there forever."

"But you heard him," Doralee reminded. "He
doesn't believe us."

"He wants to prosecute," Violet moaned.

"And he can," Doralee reasoned. "He's got you
for poisoning, me for roping him, and Judy for acting
like he's first prize at a turkey shoot."

"So how can we keep him from talking?" Judy
asked.

Violet chomped down on her sandwich. "Let's
talk about it *after* dinner. Maybe we'll be able to think
more clearly then."

After dinner, they went to the big living room and Violet sank into an overstuffed chair. Doralee found the liquor and poured three glasses of Harvey's Bristol Creme. Judy got a bright fire roaring in the fireplace. Then they lounged around, no one uttering a word, thinking, thinking hard, sprawling dejectedly on the sofas and chairs, their minds turning over and over.

Finally, Doralee broke the silence. "I say we hire a couple of wranglers to go upstairs and beat the shit out of him."

Violet's eyes rolled back in her head.

Judy wasn't listening. She had her own plan. "If we could find something on him. That's it! If we could *get* something on him, maybe we could trade off."

Violet's eyes returned to normal. "Blackmail," she said deliciously.

Judy nodded. "Both sides promise to keep their mouths shut."

Violet was enthused. "That sounds good. But what could we get on him?"

Judy was up on her knees. "A sex scandal! Get a picture of him in bed with a prostitute."

"Who'd care?" Doralee asked.

"Yeah," Violet agreed. "Hart would buy up all the copies and send them out as Christmas cards."

"Well, there has to be *something*," Judy said.

The problem was coming up with what that *something* was.

And the sun came up before an answer did.

As dawn broke through the windows, the girls were in Hart's study, going through the last of the drawers. "It's no use," Judy said. "We've gone over everything." And they had, from bedrooms to attic to cellar to den, to the laundry room, even the bathrooms. Nothing.

"Wait a minute," Violet interjected. "What's this doing here?"

"What?" Doralee asked.

Violet's expression had turned to a smile. "Well, well, well. Maybe we *do* have something to bargain with."

"What is it" Judy asked.

Violet tossed it down on the desk. "The account book for Ajax Warehouse."

"What's that mean?" Judy asked.

"If my hunch is right, it means we're free and clear." Violet grabbed the book and moved fast, "Come on, Doralee, get your coat, we're going for a ride."

Judy stayed at the house to guard Hart, while Violet and Doralee drove to a semi-deserted street on the outskirts of town and stopped at a building nestled between a lumber yard and a cement company. "This is the address," Violet said, and sure enough, there was a sign on the building. AJAX WAREHOUSE. She parked the car and got out. Doralee followed her.

"Violet, it doesn't look like a human being's been near this place in twenty years," Doralee said.

"That's the point," Violet said. She made her way to one of the windows, brushed the dust off, and peered in. "Well, I'll be damned."

Doralee did the same. "It's completely empty!"

Violet turned to her. "Yes, indeed." She rubbed her hands together in delight. "It looks like Frank has been a very naughty boy!"

Eight

"We've got the bastard now," Violet beamed, explaining to Judy what they'd discovered.

"Speaking of the bastard," Judy said, "he's complaining all his joints are hurting, being tied to the chair. Maybe we could move him to the bed and let him stretch out."

Doralee nodded, leading the way. "Sure enough. I can tie some good tight knots that'll hold him down, but'll let him be comfy."

Upstairs, they did just that, moving him to the bed and securing him there. Then Violet faced him and told him exactly what they'd found.

Hart acted as if it were nothing. "An empty warehouse. So what's wrong about that?"

"That's what Billy Sol Estes said," Violet quipped, "and they gave him fifteen years for embezzlement."

Judy was irate. "That warehouse is supposed to be full of Consolidated inventory, but you've sold it and pocketed the money! You have no ethics."

"Ha," he snorted back. Then he looked into Violet's eyes. "You'll never be able to prove any of that."

"I'll send for the invoices from the head office on Monday," she told him. "I think you'll see the light when they arrive."

"You think you're exceptionally smart, don't you?"

"Average," Violet said calmly, adding, "for a woman."

He shouted, "Well, if you start tangling with me, you'd better be prepared to play rough! Cause I'm not going to be stopped by three dumb-witted broads."

"How dare you?" Doralee hissed.

"I'm getting out of here," he yelled, kicking, pulling angrily on the ropes with his hands. "I'm breaking out of here, even if I have to kill you three to do it." He began to gnaw on the rope holding his right hand.

Violet looked to Doralee.

Doralee looked to Judy.

Judy nodded.

As they walked down the stairs again, Violet said, "If we're going to keep him tied up for three or four days, we've got to devise a better system of confinement. It'll take that long for the invoices to come through, and that's the hard evidence."

Doralee thought for a moment. "I got it. Come on, we're going to a pet store."

"Thinking of buying a dog to keep him company?" Violet asked in her low register.

Judy said, "Better one to eat him."

"Don't ask questions," Doralee said, half out the door already, "just come on."

The sign said PET AND SADDLE SUPPLY and the girls entered and looked around. Violet and Judy went over to the dog collars and checked them out. On the way, Doralee had explained they needed some kind of leather restraint, which would keep him bound. Violet showed Judy a dog collar with big silver studs in it.

Judy shook her head. "It should be something comfortable. Something that keeps him restrained, but gives him a certain freedom of movement. These are for taking Fido for a walk."

"Come over here," Doralee called. She was fingering a leather harness. "My mama used to keep us kids on a leash with a cut-down old mule harness that strapped in the back."

"That doesn't sound *too* unpleasant," Judy said.

"*She* survived it," Violet added.

Judy looked at Doralee's marvelous figure. "Pretty well, in fact. Maybe *we* should have had mule harnesses when we were kids."

Doralee laughed. "Stop fooling around, this is serious."

"This is ridiculous," Violet interjected.

Judy thought about it. "Hmm. We could find some handcuffs that are easy on the skin. Then, with the harness, he would be sufficiently restrained."

"Better than hog-tied!" Doralee sang.

Back in the car, Violet said, "We've got to board up those windows in the bedroom. We can't chance him poking a perfume bottle through one and yelling across the neighborhood." She started the car and moved into traffic. "I think the next stop should be a hardware store."

"There's one on the next block," Doralee said. "They've got everything."

As they walked into the hardware store, Doralee said, "You know, we'll have to move the furniture from his reach."

Violet stopped and shook her head. "How are we going to keep him secure? I mean, what's he going to be hooked to?"

Judy remembered an ad she saw for an Army surplus store. "How about buying a parachute rig and hanging him from the ceiling."

But Violet had a better idea. There, on the far wall, she spied something she knew all about, seeing that she'd just installed one herself. "I know, I got it. We hook him to a wire from the ceiling. With a garage-door opener."

"Wonderful!" Doralee said.

"You got it!" Judy added.

They ordered plywood, gathered up weights and pulleys and springs and yards of chain. At the front counter, Violet said, "We'd also like your best garage-door opener, please."

"Absolutely, ma'am." The clerk called to a stockboy. "Jim, get these ladies' a big 704." He said to Violet, "It'll be right up. I'll total your bill."

"What do you say?" Violet asked the others. "You think we can pull it off?"

"As long as he's comfortable," Judy said, nodding.

"I think it's delightful," Doralee said, "because all this is his own fault."

The clerk interrupted. "Will that be all?"

"Yes," Doralee said, reaching into her purse. "I'd like to put it on Master Charge, please."

"Yes, ma'am, *Mrs. Hart*," he said, reading the name from the plastic card she handed him, "I'll write it up real quick."

"You do that, honey."

Frank Hart sat in his underwear in the middle of his bed, a dog collar around his neck and a leather harness secured over his chest and under his arms. Various chains and pulleys were attached to hooks in the ceiling beams. Violet had just finished the last of the installation of the garage-door opener above the bed. She then hooked a three-pronged cable running down his back to the opener on the ceiling. "Smile," Violet said. "Soon you're going to be Peter Pan."

She got a fan from another bedroom and plugged it in near the bed. "We figure you'll sign our statement by the end of the week," Violet said. "And then we'll let you go."

"This is inhumane," he hissed. "Torture. I'm being held hostage."

"Count your lucky stars you got us and not some crazy terrorists."

Hart blinked. Was she *serious?* God Almighty, they were all cuckoo. *Oh, Jesus, here comes the other one.*

Doralee entered from the bathroom. "I've got all the razors and scissors and I removed the glass, just in case."

Judy came in from the hall. "I brought you some

books and magazines," she said, dumping them next to him on the bed. "This is a good one." She held up a copy of *Soap Opera Digest*. "It'll keep you up on the daytime shows. You ever watch 'General Hospital?' Once your start, they really hook you."

Violet looked around. "Well, it's a little sparse in here with some of the furniture gone, and I'll admit the sunlight made it more cheerful, but your wife has good taste in decor. It won't be *too* unpleasant."

"Shit," Hart muttered.

"Judy will be staying here at night," Violet explained. "Doralee will be bringing your lunch. And during the day we have this security system." She pointed to the garage-door opener.

"You three are nuts!" he shouted. "Completely crazy! You think you can keep me here for a whole week? For Chrissakes, I'm the boss—don't you think I might be missed at the office?"

They looked at each other and smiled.

They'd already taken care of that.

On Monday morning, Doralee sat at her desk as usual. Behind her, the company maintenance man was putting in a new pane of glass in Hart's door. The phone rang. "Franklin Hart's office. No, he's out right now. Can I help? Yes, Mr. Strell, I'll ask him about that and I'm sure he'll get back to you." She hung up and jotted a note to herself.

Bob Enright walked up. "Hi, Doralee. Is he in?"

"Not right now, Bob. I'm sorry."

"He said on Friday he wanted to see me first thing today."

"He did?" She thought for a moment. "Oh, yes. He told me to tell you to forget about it."

"Oh?"

"Yes, he just wanted you to know what a great job you're doing."

Bob seemed very pleased. "He said that? Wow. He's not the kind to pass out compliments. Thanks, Doralee. You're a peach."

She smiled as he walked away. "I know it." Then the phone rang again. "Franklin Hart's office. Yes, Roz. I'm holding all his calls. Sorry." She listened to Roz protesting. "I realize you want to speak to him today, but if *he* isn't speaking to anyone, how are you going to talk to him? Okay, I'll tell him, but don't count on it. He's very busy today."

Violet walked up. "How's it going?"

"*She's* going to be tough," Doralee said, putting the phone down.

"Let me guess. Our Lady of the Stalls?"

"Yup."

"How about the others?"

"Piece of cake." She handed Violet the pad on which she'd made notes. "Here are some questions Strell wants answered."

Violet glanced at them. "No problem, I can handle this."

"And you'd better see these letters." She handed Violet a stack of mail. "How about some coffee?"

Violet shot her a look.

"Whoops," Doralee giggled. "Sorry."

All morning long, Doralee fended off callers and took notes on questions for Hart's decision. At break time, she got together with Violet and Judy and they discussed the decisions that had to be made. Violet had enough experience with the company to come up with the answers. And Doralee knew precisely how to make them sound as if they came straight from Hart himself. "I'm a better horse's mouth than the horse's mouth," she remarked.

Judy looked at her watch. "I wonder if Hart is watching 'Ryan's Hope' or 'Search for Tomorrow.'"

"Did you have any trouble with Dwayne?" Violet asked Doralee.

"No. Just told him we had a load of work and with Hart out for a few days, I'd be very busy."

"Good. I told my kids Judy was sick and I'd be having to care for her off and on."

"I *am* sick," Judy replied. "Anyone who'd agree to spend the entire night at Franklin Hart's house . . ."

"His wife has done it for eighteen years," Doralee put in.

"Yeah," Violet added. "And look what it's done to her. She checked out years ago."

"Well, time to go back and be the collective Frank Hart." Doralee got up from the lunch table. "You know, I feel kinda powerful."

"Like it?" Judy asked.

Doralee grinned. "Love it."

"Irma, tell Mr. Strell that Mr. Hart dictated a memo on the Freling inquiry and that Mr. Strell should get it in the morning. Thanks. Bye." Doralee put the phone down to find Roz standing in front of her desk.

"Is Mr. Hart in?"

Doralee smiled sweetly and said, "I believe so. Go on in."

"Thank you." Roz turned, feeling important again, and entered Hart's office. It was empty. She went to his private bathroom door and knocked discreetly. "Mr. Hart, are you in there?" No answer. Roz looked perplexed. She called to Doralee. "He isn't *here!*"

Doralee came in. "Did you try the john?"

"He's not in there either."

"That's funny," Doralee said, feigning amazement. "Well, he hasn't gone to lunch yet—his coat is still here." She pointed to the jacket she'd brought with her from the house. "And look—I've told him a hundred times that's very dangerous." She grabbed the burning cigar in the ash tray and snuffed it out. "I'm sure he'll be back. Would you like to wait?"

"No, thank you. But please tell him it's still very important I talk to him sometime this afternoon, all right?"

"Sure, honey."

Doralee carried Hart's lunch up the stairs. Pastrami on rye with extra mustard, a crunchy pickle, and a Tab. "Mr. Hart, I'm here with some food!"

He heard her coming and prepared his plan. All morning long he'd thought about what to do. Now he was ready. He'd searched the room for something to use as a weapon, but came up with nothing—until he looked around the bathroom. Under the vanity was a wooden stool, which either escaped notice or had not been considered threatening.

He had smashed the stool against the tile wall until it splintered, and then yanked one of the legs off. It was nice and heavy. Felt good in his hand. Would crack one of them nicely over the skull. He made sure it was hidden at his side under the covers. Then he ran his fingers through his hair and waited for Doralee to open the door.

"Hi."

"Hi."

"I brought lunch. Sorry it's so late, but there's been a lot of work to do." She set her purse down on the dressing table.

"Work to do!" He was enraged. "For who?"

"You, of course. You don't think just because you're not there, the place is going to come to a standstill, do you?" She opened the sack, spread out the sandwich and popped open the Tab. "And everything is going nicely, so you don't have to worry." She pushed the bed stand closer to him, to use as a lunch table. "In fact, no one misses you. Eat your pickle."

He narrowed his eyes and said nothing. She turned and went to her purse. *Now,* he told himself.

Doralee dug into her purse. "I brought a couple cookies from a batch Betty brought to work." She looked up and caught a flash in the mirror, Hart standing at the side of the bed, a chunk of wood in his hand raised to strike her. Quickly, without a moment's hesitation, she dropped her purse and smashed her hand down on the Magic Wand.

The machine went into gear. Hart was jerked back, up over the bed, kicking and bouncing like a reluctant marionette. "Son of a bitch!" he hollered "You're gonna pay for this, Doralee!"

"Oh, by the way," she said, walking over to his food, "Roz wants to talk to you sometime today. I told her I'd be sure to give you the message." She took a bite of the pickle, looked up at Hart swinging from the ceiling, and smiled. It was a warm, friendly smile.

"I don't understand," a perturbed Roz said between her teeth. "Did you give him my message?"

"Yes, I did." Doralee was calmly doing her nails at her desk. "I told him, just as you asked, but he walked out just a second ago. Maybe you can catch him." She swung around in her chair and shouted down the hall. "Judy, can you see Mr. Hart?"

Judy, who just *happened* to be standing at the end of the hall, looked, and answered. "Yes."

"Stop him."

Judy rushed to the elevators. "Mr. Hart, oh, Mr. Hart!"

Roz took off in pursuit of Judy, while Doralee went back to filing her nails.

As Roz rounded the corner, Judy said, "Now!"

Violet, positioned inside the elevator, punched the *UP* button and the doors shut just as Roz came up to them. "Sorry," Judy said, "you just missed him."

Roz kicked at the elevator doors. "Damn!"

Everyone left at five. But Judy and Doralee were camped out in Hart's office, nestled into the sofa with their feet up, waiting for Violet. "How'd Roz take it?" Doralee asked.

"Pissed," Judy replied. "We can't keep that kind of thing up all week. We'll wear ourselves out, and besides, she's going to get suspicious very soon."

"You're right. She's going to be a problem."

Violet joined them. "I've got some bad news. Here's the Telex from the New York office." She handed it to them. "They've started the computer changeover and they won't be able to send us the inventory invoices on Ajax Warehouse for another four to six weeks."

Judy gasped. "Four to six weeks!"

"My God," Doralee moaned, sinking further into the couch.

"Do we have to keep Hart tied up all that time?" Judy asked.

Violet sat on his desk. "Do we have a choice?"

"I think we could pull it off," Doralee said. "I never realized how unpopular Hart is. No one wants to see him face to face if they can help it. They're all loving it that I'm giving them his answers over the phone, instead of him calling them in to see him."

"Everyone except Roz," Judy muttered.

Doralee sat up straight. "Hey, I've got it. Send Hart on vacation. Tell everyone he's gone to meet his wife in the South Seas."

Violet shook her head. "No. We'd have to get Hinkle to okay that. I think we'll be all right if we keep everything on this floor."

Judy said, "There's got to be an answer, then." She got up and walked around. Violet took off her shoes and rubbed her feet. "I know," Judy said, excited. "Why don't we send *Roz* on vacation?"

Violet's eyes brightened.

Doralee's positively sparkled. "Now you're talking!"

"That's wonderful, Judy," Violet said.

"I'll type it up," Doralee said. "She deserves a rest."

"Sure does," Judy added. "And we need one from her."

Violet looked at the calendar on Hart's wall. "The most we could ditch her for is two weeks. We've got to keep her away longer than that. What can we do?"

"I don't know, but we'll think of something." Judy picked up her purse. "We can discuss it tonight. I think we'd better get going. After what he tried to do at lunch time, we shouldn't leave him alone longer than necessary."

"Right," Doralee said. "I'll get my coat."

"I'm on my way." Violet slipped on her shoes and followed them out the door.

The trio were gathered in Hart's study discussing the problem of Roz.

Judy was checking the books on the shelves. One of them was *Basic French*. "Hey, have you ever heard of the Aspen Language Center?"

Doralee shook her head.

"Nope," Violet said.

"It's where they do that concentrated immersion in a foreign language. How about we send old Roz there?"

Violet liked it. "That's not bad. Not bad at all."

"But how do we pull it off?" Doralee asked.

Violet volunteered. "We could have Hart write her that it's top secret, something real important and hush-hush."

"She'll love it," Judy said.

"Tell her Consolidated is opening overseas centers," Violet continued, "and they need executives who can speak another language."

"What will we give her?" Doralee asked.

Judy held up the French book.

"What the hell?" Violet said. "Why not?"

"Do you think she'll go?" Judy asked.

"Are you kidding?" Doralee responded with a hoot. "If Hart asked her to, she'd go to Africa and learn Swahili!"

Judy flopped back on the sofa. "Ladies, I think we've got it made."

Two days later, Doralee ran into the ladies' room, where Judy and Violet were waiting for her. "I checked the stalls," Violet said.

"She got it!" Doralee waved a letter from Roz "formally" accepting Hart's request "with honor." "It was so easy. I just typed a memo and signed his name to it."

Judy asked, "Did you tell her he wasn't going to be able to talk to her about it in person?"

"Yup. I said, 'Because of the secret nature of this assignment, it would not be proper for us to discuss it until after the language training has been completed. Company spies, jealousy, you know.'"

Violet howled. "She sure does."

"How long are we getting rid of her for?" Judy asked.

"She won't be back until the fifteenth," Doralee replied.

Judy asked, "When does Mrs. Hart return?"

"The twenty-fourth," Doralee answered. "Poor Missy, I feel sorry for her. I think I'll have Hart send her some flowers in Tahiti."

"That would be a nice touch," Violet said. "Well, we've done it, we've got the time now. When does the battle-ax depart?"

"I ordered the plane ticket," Doralee said. "Tomorrow morning at seven."

"I'll breathe easier," Violet said, "when I know she's in the sky...."

The bathroom door opened and Roz walked in.

The girls froze.

"Bonjour," Roz said.

Nine

Judy was doing the dinner dishes in Hart's kitchen, while Doralee and Violet prepared a large calendar showing the six weeks they'd have to keep him confined. Judy finished the pans, and then filled the dishwasher with detergent and punched a button. "You know, I'm going to miss this place when we have to leave."

"How was he when you took the tray up?" Violet asked.

"Very subdued. He's plotting something."

"Probably good for him to keep his mind occupied," Doralee said.

Violet nodded. "I guess it's going to be a race to see if he can get free before we receive the inventory invoices around"—she looked at the calendar and marked a big red "X" where her calculations told her it should go—"there."

Judy joined them at the table. She sipped the coffee Violet had poured for her. "Mmm. What kind tonight?"

"Bavarian Chocolate," Violet answered. "Missy has it sent in from Macy's in New York. Not a bad way to live. All I ever do is open a can of Maxwell House."

Judy smiled. "I *am* going to miss this place." She took a bite of the brownies they'd found frozen in the ice box. "One thing this experience has taught me, I've got to get a coffee grinder and crush my own beans."

"That's profound," Violet said with a smile.

Judy winked. "Doralee, did you ever send those flowers, speaking of Missy Hart?"

"Sure did. Went hog-wild. Even dictated a nice mushy note from him." She saw the sudden worry in Violet's eyes. "No, nothing out of character . . ." Then she whispered. "I'll tell you, you'd be embarrassed to hear the way he talks to her sometimes, Missy-Missy, Sweetie Pie . . . ugh."

Violet perked her ears. "Uh-oh. He's kicking again."

"Just blowing off steam," Judy said.

But Doralee was pondering something. "You know, sending those flowers has got me thinking. With Roz gone too, we could make a few changes, brighten up the old office. I'm thinking of having Hart allow people to keep flowers on their desks. Wouldn't that be nice?"

"Nice?" Judy toasted with her coffee cup. "It would be positively glorious!"

"He's got to make some changes in the office. Some of those rules of his are so depressing," Doralee said.

"Photos should be allowed," Violet said. "Let the workers personalize their desks a little."

"Sure," Judy said, "pictures of husbands and wives, friends, lovers, dogs and cats."

Doralee said, "Maybe something in the halls. Brighten everyone up. Old movie posters or something."

"We could have Hart get a memo off to maintenance to paint the lunch room yellow," Violet said. "Or beige with big flower prints. Rainbows. Anything but that horrible diarrhea-green."

"I have this special poem by Rod McKuen," Doralee said. "I'd love to post it behind my desk."

"If we're going to do all that," Violed suggested, "why not make some changes that *really* count."

"Yes," Judy said. "Like people getting the same salary for doing the same job."

Doralee started taking notes. "And how about letting people know when a job's become available."

"Right, some fairness for a change." Judy thought more. "Maybe job-sharing and staggered hours."

Violet leaned back in the chair. "Now you're talking." Then she looked up at the ceiling and cackled, "Are your ears burning, Frank?"

Enormous changes occurred on the sixteenth floor during the next few weeks. Each day, the workers gathered around the newly installed bulletin board, reading the latest memo from a boss nobody had seen for a while, but whom they were growing to love.

Flowers and plants appeared on desks. Photos of families, boyfriends and girlfriends, dogs and cats, even parakeets, monkeys and turtles. Poems and quotations, posters of sunsets and towering pine trees, blow-ups of movie and rock stars lined the walls. The lunch room was now a cheery yellow, painted by Tom Wood who had confessed to being a Sunday artist. Tom had also painted graphic sunflowers with huge pale leaves to highlight the decor. Business in the company restaurant had doubled.

But the changes were more than cosmetic. The entire atmosphere changed. People smiled more. There were fewer problems, fewer arguments, even fewer mistakes in typing and filing. The new sense of freedom and warmth amidst a still strong office schedule made for increased productivity and an all-around happier and healthier environment.

One evening at five, several of the secretaries gathered around the bulletin board. There was a new memo announcing that on Monday, a new salary plan would become reality, and all pay would be based on work done, with *no* discrimination.

Margaret Foster said to Violet, "Never thought I'd live to see the day. What's come over the old coot?"

"Don't know," Violet said in reply, "I guess he finally found his heart."

At that moment, Franklin Hart was pacing back and forth in the little space in front of his bed.

The chains clanked behind him. "Gotta get out," he said, "gotta get out, gotta get out." He was a crazed prisoner, determined and intent. "Gotta get out, gotta get out," he chanted, but then finally fell back onto the mattress, pounding his fists and kicking his feet like a child throwing a tantrum.

When it subsided, he said out loud, "Must be calm, must be calm. Gotta think, gotta think." He stared at the TV set. Then looked at the time. The soaps were over, but it was just about time for Mary Tyler Moore. He picked up the remote control unit and pressed it, but his thumb hit two buttons at once, and all of a sudden he heard a familiar chugging.

The TV didn't turn on.

But the garage-door opener had.

"Oh, no!" he screamed. "Shit, no!"

He zipped off into the air.

Doralee had mailed a letter from "Hart" the first day they'd begun implementing the changes, and now as a result of that letter, Maria Delgrado had returned to work. Charlotte Whitherspoon presented Maria with a bouquet of flowers for her desk, and Maria, in tears, said, "I can't thank you all enough, it's wonderful to be back." Then she looked around. "But can this be the same place I used to work?"

At one o'clock the same day, Barbara Adams took over for Lee Chang for the rest of the afternoon. Job-sharing was now "officially" in effect.

"A whole week and a half," Violet said, crossing off another day on the calendar. "Without a hitch."

"The best week this company's had in its history," Doralee announced. "You know, it's strange, sometimes I actually think *he's* doing all this. Sometimes when I see him up there, I want to say thank you. Isn't that nutty?"

"I know what you mean," Judy said. "You almost believe he's really in that office, making everything better. People actually *like* him now."

"That's 'cause they don't have to look at him," Violet interjected.

Doralee laughed. "No one misses that old puss of his, that's for sure."

Judy stirred cream into her Jamaican High Mountain, fresh from Missy Hart's loaded freezer. "What amazes me is that it is all so easy."

"Thank God for Hinkle giving the boss of each floor autonomy," Violet said.

"Just goes to show," Doralee said, "that kind of power can be used democratically or as a dictator."

"Reminds me," Violet said, "we didn't give Papa Doc any dessert tonight. Think he'd like some apple tarts. I spied some at the back of the freezer."

"I don't know about him," Doralee said, "but I'd love some."

"Coming right up."

As Violet prepared the tarts, Judy and Doralee went to the living room and stretched out in front of the fireplace. Doralee had her note pad ready. "You know, paint is chipping all over the locker room."

"I avoid that place at all costs. It's so ugly and depressing. And it stinks in there."

"Think I should type up a memo?"

Judy nodded. "Absolutely. And have Hart *specifically* request Tom Wood this time—"

"And I'll have him *insist* on paying for his services."

"Right. I know Tom loved doing the kitchen, but there's no reason he shouldn't get paid for his talent."

Doralee jotted it down. "What else?"

"The storage room."

"What about it?"

"It's a dungeon."

"A pit."

Judy seemed a little apprehensive. "I fear this may be asking too much. . . ."

"Try. The worst he can do is say no."

Judy nodded. "Well, Maria was telling me today

how sometimes she can't find a baby-sitter and she has to pay so much for an expensive one that it doesn't pay to work. And some days she'll have to leave early just because of the sitter's schedule."

"Hmm."

"I was thinking . . . well . . . what if there was a day-care center for children of the workers . . . nearby."

"How nearby?" Doralee asked.

"As nearby as the storage room?"

"Hmm." She thought about it. Then she called out, "Violet, you know that filthy storage room where they keep the broken typewriters?"

"Yeah," Violet yelled from the kitchen.

"Judy thinks we should turn it into a day-care room for kids."

"Get it painted first," Violet shouted.

Judy put her arms around Doralee. "Oh, I'm so thrilled. It will mean so much to so many of the secretaries. And it'll make work easier."

"I know. So many of the women worry about their kids during the day, especially those with little ones who aren't in school yet."

"There's a girl in section four who used to be a nurse's aide in pediatrics. I wonder if she'd want to give up filing for taking care of the kids?"

"Why'd she quit nursing?" Doralee asked.

"Money. She makes more as a file clerk. But she hates doing it, of course."

Doralee wrote herself a note. "Well, then, she'll get paid the same thing she's getting now, only she'll be doing something she likes."

Judy leaned forward and looked into the fire. "Doralee, I can't begin to tell you how good I feel about this. I thought my life was coming to an end that day Dick told me he was going off to Mexico with Lisa. But it was only the beginning. For the first time, ever, I'm doing something that's really *good*."

"We're helping bring things around the way they should be in the first place," Doralee said.

Violet entered, taking her apron off. "They're in

the oven." She sat down. "What depresses me is that
he's really going to be back one day and then everything we've done to help will get reversed."

"Maybe we can include that in the bargain with
him," Judy said. "Make him promise not to change a
thing."

"After attempted murder, humiliation, kidnapping
and all the rest, I doubt that we can expect much
more." Violet stared into the fire. "It is wonderful,
though, isn't it? For the first time in the twelve years
I've been there, everyone loves their work."

"We can't think about him coming back,"
Doralee said. "We'll cross that bridge another time,
when we get there. Right now, let's toast to the day-
care center." She jumped up and got a bottle of brandy
and poured three glasses. "I can already see the sign
that Tom will paint. *Day Care Center*. With little
bears and tigers around it. It's gonna be wonderful!"

"And all because of good old Frank." Judy
toasted.

"To good old Frank." Doralee clicked her glass
against Judy's.

Violet did the same. "To F. Hart," she said.

"Gotta think, gotta think, gotta think," F. Hart
repeated, sounding deranged. Then an idea struck him.
The fan. The stupid fan they put in there for him to get
some air. He moved himself in a position where he
could get it unplugged from the wall, and then he
ripped the cord out of the back of it.

He picked up the pitcher of water from the bed-
side table and dumped it all over the carpet in front of
the door. Then he frayed the wires at the end of the
cord and stuck it into the wet carpet. He held the plug
in his hand, sitting next to the outlet by the bed,
waiting for the first one of them who would have the
bad luck to walk in.

He sat there for twenty minutes.

Then he heard something. Which one was it?
"*...a surprise dessert for you!*" Doralee! Good, she
deserved it before the other two anyhow, she's the one

who should have been the most loyal. Yeah, give her a taste of her own medicine—

He heard her opening the door.

This is it, Mrs Rhodes. The jig is up. He held the plug directly in front of the holes in the outlet.

She entered.

He looked up. She was carrying a plate with some kind of steaming pastry on it. Well, she'd carry it straight to heaven. He let out a howl of delight, and shoved the plug into the wall.

Sparks flew. But from the socket, not the other end of the cord at Doralee's feet. The electricity shot through Hart's body, up through his chains, and the jolt activated the apparatus on the ceiling. He was flung into the air like a parachutist caught in a tree.

Doralee shook her head. She set the apple tart on the table, and then pushed the remote control switch and let him down. He hit the bed with a thump.

She shrugged, turned, and walked out.

The next day, employees gathered at the bulletin board as Doralee posted the latest memo from their boss, the announcement of the Day Care Center. Everyone cheered. Everyone but a thin man with an angular face, an odd-looking person who was taking notes, but was unnoticed by anyone. As Doralee went back to her desk to call the painters and maintenance men to clean out the storage room, the thin man watched her closely, wrote something down, and disappeared on the elevator.

Doralee opened the morning's mail to find a note from Missy to her husband, thanking him for the lovely flowers. She included a photo of herself standing under a palm tree. She looked very happy in her white sunglasses, pedal pushers and tennis shoes.

Doralee picked up the phone. "Honey, get me that florist I talked to last time. Yeah. I want to order more flowers to be sent to"—she checked Missy's itinerary—"Hawaii."

At five, the women gathered in Hart's office as usual. "How'd it go?" Violet asked.

"Wonderful," Judy said. "They started cleaning out the dungeon already."

"Painters are coming tomorrow," Doralee told her.

"Great." Violet went behind Hart's desk and looked at the phone. "Ready?"

"If you are," Doralee said.

Judy nodded and went to the extension near the sofa. "All set."

"When you see the light go on, pick up." With that, Doralee left for her desk.

A few moments later, Judy and Violet were listening in on Doralee's conversation. . . .

". . . Mr. Hart so wanted to call you himself, Roz, but he's in a meeting with Mr. Hinkle, so he asked me to be sure to do it. But after five, so no one else would hear. It's still top secret, you understand."

"Doralee, you caught me in the middle of practicing tomorrow's lesson. Listen to this: *Voici ma plume . . .*"

Violet covered the mouthpiece and sucked in her breath.

"Voici ma libre . . ."

Judy held up a warning finger.

"Voici mon béret!"

Violet had to put the receiver down. She doubled up in laughter, and fell from Hart's chair, howling. "I can see her standing there, slapping her fat hand on her silly beret . . . oh, God, spare me!"

"Doralee, what's that I heard?"

"Nothing, Roz. Interference on the line. Listen, I'll be sure to tell Mr. Hart exactly what you told me. Glad to hear everything is going so well for you. Bye."

"Au revoir," Roz sang.

Doralee dropped the phone. "I love it, I love it, I love it!" she screamed.

"I hate it, I hate it, I hate it," Hart muttered. He looked desperate. Haggard. Tormented.

He went to his bathroom, searching the drawers

for the hundredth time. Each was empty and each depressed him more.

He thought he heard a sound from outside. His hearing was becoming more and more acute now that most of his senses were restricted. Yes, he did hear something. He went to the boarded window where a week ago he'd discovered a slight crack which gave him a good view of the driveway. It was easy to make out the driveway, even in the dark, because the streetlight afforded him a good view. It was Judy's car—but he noticed the figure of a man hiding behind the neighbor's tree at the front of the drive, far from the house. The man seemed to be watching the car and casing the house. Hart stiffened. Good God, that's all he needed, to be robbed on top of everything else. The man disappeared in the trees, and Hart turned away.

He returned to the bathroom and continued to search the drawers. Some intuition was telling him there was hope in there. He found a half-used bar of Camay. No, he couldn't do anything with that. No, there had to be something more—

There it was. In the cabinet behind the place where Missy kept the toilet paper. A metal nail file. A little rusty, but still strong. He picked it up and smiled gleefully at his good fortune.

Judy brought Hart's dinner tray up to him. "There's a man out there," he said to her.

"Out where?" She set the tray down and popped open a Tab.

"In front of the house. He's going to rob me, I know it."

"Sure."

"But I tell you, I saw him."

"Sure, sure. Just give a yell when you're done."

"You're the one who's going to yell," he shouted over his mashed potatoes. "When you're getting raped and murdered down there, don't you come yelling to me. I'll be able to say then, *I told you so!*"

She shrugged and went out the door.

He ate quickly, then went back to working at filing his leather wristband with the rusty nail file. It was slow going, but what else did he have to do that was pressing? He went at it like a demon possessed, and in a while he'd sawed through half of it. And he smiled for the first time in a long time.

It was dark now, and very windy outside. Judy could hear it whistling through the window panes. She wished Hart hadn't said those things about rape and murder. She was starting to get the creeps. As she loaded the dishwasher, she started humming a song to herself, to take her mind off it. Then, after punching the start button, she turned off the kitchen lights, then went through the downstairs, doing the same to each room.

Outside, the eyes followed her through the windows, watching her every move.

She stopped in the study and checked the bookshelves. She decided on *Cashelmara,* a book she remembered Charlotte reading voraciously on her breaks at work. Then, just as she was going to sit down, she screamed.

The figure of a man was outlined through the French doors. He rapped on the glass and Judy dropped the book and ran behind the sofa. Then, recovering a little, she saw that the face was familiar. Very familiar, as a matter of fact. "My God," she breathed, getting up to open the door for him. "Dick! What are you doing here?"

Ten

"It's cold out here," Dick Radman said. "Can I come in?"

She let him in and closed the door. "I thought you were in Mexico."

"I was. I came back." He seemed nervous.

"What for?"

"Long story." He sat down.

"Dick," she said with a look of slight panic, "you can't stay."

"You're here alone, aren't you?"

She blinked. "Yes. I'm . . . I'm house-sitting for a friend."

"Yeah. I've been casing the place for the last few days to make sure." He rubbed his hands together. "Come on, you could spare a cup of coffee for your freezing old husband, couldn't you?"

"Ex-husband," she corrected. "I suppose so. But then you'll really have to go."

He followed her to the kitchen, where the coffee machine was still hot. She poured two mugs, and they went back to the study. "Not a bad place your friend's got here," Dick said.

"It's okay."

Dick sat on the couch. "Listen, Judy, it was no good from the start. Nothing worked. Lisa left after the first week."

"I'm really sorry."

"I got a job."

"Well, that's good."

"A waiter in a resort hotel."

She could hardly believe it. No, the truth was, she could believe it. Looking back, she saw many weaknesses in him that she'd never allowed herself to face. "I'm really sorry, Dick. Really I am." And she was, but the important thing was to get him out of the house. All she needed was for him to stick around long enought to hear Hart banging away with one of his schemes to get free. "Maybe if I call you—no, you call me tomorrow at work. We can have lunch together and talk about it then."

He looked into her eyes. "I've wanted to see you, Judy. I followed you from the office. I thought maybe you were living with someone."

"No. No."

"Judy, I've really needed to see you, talk to you. I was afraid to face you at first. I thought maybe I'd ruined your life."

"My life is wonderful, Dick." She stood up. "Let's talk about it tomorrow. You'd really better go now. I'm not supposed to have visitors here. After ten, that is."

Then there was a thump on the ceiling.

"What was that?" Dick asked.

"Nothing. Probably the cat. I'd better check." She started to hurry out of the room.

"I'll go with you."

She stopped dead and turned to him. "No! I mean, it's all right, I won't be a second. Sit down and relax."

He took her hand. "Judy."

"What?"

"You look as beautiful as ever."

"Thanks." She shook his hand and ran out of the study and up the stairs.

When she opened the door to the bedroom, she understood what the thud had been. Hart had somehow gotten a cuff open, and when it snapped, the chain flew up and off its pulley and one of the wall weights fell to the floor. "Oh, my God," Judy cried as she looked into the room. Hart, with one hand free, was trying to get himself untied and unchained.

She dashed for the bed and pulled with all her might on one of the still-secured chains against the wall. It unbalanced Hart and swung him up by one foot. "Let me down!" he called. "Leave that alone— get away!"

"Quiet, be quiet," she begged.

He lashed out at her, but she had the advantage —it was easy to keep him there by holding onto the chain with only one hand. With the other, she grabbed the linen napkin she'd brought up at dinner and stuffed it into his mouth. Then she clipped a wire onto the back of his harness and pulled another rope attached to the pulley, then hit the lever, and he slammed up against the ceiling, kicking, struggling, sputtering, back in suspension.

Judy ran out of the room and slammed the door behind her just as Dick reached the landing.

"What's going on?"

Judy held her back against the door. "Nothing."

"Who's in that room?"

"Nobody."

Dick narrowed his eyes. He heard muffled cries from behind the door. "Judy—"

"Come on, let's go downstairs," she said. "You can tell me all about the Acapulco Hilton."

He wouldn't let her pass. "Judy, there's someone in that room."

"No there isn't."

"Let me see."

"No."

He shoved her side and flung the door open. His mouth dropped as he laid eyes on a struggling man in his underwear, hanging in chairs over the bed. "Good God!" Dick gasped.

Judy pulled him back and slammed the door. "You didn't see that."

"Who . . ." He could barely talk he was so shocked "Who was that?"

"A friend."

"Obviously." He put it together. "So that's what you're into now? Bondage?"

"What's that?"

"Bondage! S&M. Sex games, you know, a little leather, a little pain—"

"Yeah!" she said, realizing he'd just come up with the finest explanation in the world. "That's right, I'm into everything now. All of it." She began to hustle him down the stairs. "Come on, get out of here, I've got a great evening ahead of me."

Dick walked down the stairs in a kind of trance. "I can't believe it—who is that guy, anyway?"

"He's my boss."

"Your boss? You're having an affair with your boss? Isn't that typical?"

She walked ahead of him on the first floor, leading him to the front door. "Yeah, just like you having an affair with your secretary."

"But we didn't play any sicko games. Judy, this isn't you, you can't be serious—"

"Don't tell me what I can and can't do!" she screamed at him. "Those days are over. If I want to have an affair and play sex games and do M&M's, you can't stop me!"

"M&M's?"

Then she hit him with the whopper: "As a matter of fact, I smoke pot."

"What?" He looked stunned.

"Pot! Pot, you jerk! It means marijuana!"

"I know what it means. And I can see what that kind of living has done to you."

"I've changed," she said, proudly, defiantly.

"I'll say! And not for the better." He leaned up against the mahogany-paneled wall of the foyer. "And to think I actually came here tonight to ask you to come back to me."

"Fat chance!" she bellowed. "Go back to what? Your leaving was the best thing that ever happened to me."

He shrugged. "If that's the way you feel, there's nothing more to say."

"Oh yes there is," she growled, swinging open the massive door. "Hit the road, buster! This is where you get off."

Dick stepped outside and she slammed the door behind him.

Judy got up bright and early, had breakfast and took a shower, and then brought a tray to Hart and said good-bye to him for the day. She hopped in her car and drove out of the driveway, not even noticing the cab coming up the street.

The cab turned into the same driveway, and pulled up to the front door. A woman got out of the backseat, wearing Hawaiian leis around her neck and sporting a coconut palm hat. "Just cart everything into the hall," she told the driver, handing him a fifty-dollar bill, "I have to go see if my Franklin's still home, my sweet husband. . . ."

Missy climbed the stairs to the bedroom. The door was shut. Perhaps she was early enough, perhaps he'd overslept. She knocked three times at the door, smiling, and then slowly pushed it open.

He lay there in his chains and ropes, crunching on an English muffin, watching the "Today" show. The muffin fell from his mouth. "Missy?" he moaned, as if she were an apparition, a mirage.

She put her hands to her hips and scrunched up her little nose. "Frank, what on earth are you up to?"

He looked at her with as much surprise as she was looking at him.

In the Downtowner Coffee Shoppe, Judy sat at a table with Doralee, finishing lunch. "So what are we going to do about Roz?" Judy asked. "She gets back Friday."

Doralee stabbed the last of her chef's salad with the fork. "Well, if she starts giving us any trouble, we can always send her back and have her learn German."

Violet came running. "Oh, am I glad I found you two! I just spoke to New York—we'll have the invoices here first thing Friday morning!"

"Hooray!" Doralee squealed.

"Then we don't have to worry about Roz at all," Judy said. "I was just telling Doralee what happened last night. I'm glad it's almost over."

A waitress brought over a white paper plate covered with another white paper plate. "What's that?" Violet asked.

"Hart's lunch. Gotta take it there now," Doralee said, going into her purse for money. "Thought a tuna melt would be a nice little treat."

Judy just thought of something. "Doralee, you keep paying for all his food. Why don't you let us chip in something?"

"You think *I'm* paying for his calories? You kidding?" Doralee pulled out a twenty and laid it on the check. "It comes out of petty cash. He puts in a request every Monday. He's buying his own food."

"I love it," Violet said, finishing the last of Doralee's Coke. "You know what's given me the most pleasure?"

"What?" Judy asked.

"The fact that we've been able to bring him coffee with real sugar, regular old white sugar in it, and he's had no choice but to drink it!"

Doralee got up. "Gotta run, see you two later. . . ." She grabbed the tuna melt and was off.

Doralee entered the big house and set her purse on the kitchen counter. She opened the plates, stuck the food in the microwave for a moment, and then put it on a tray and grabbed a can of Coke from the refrigerator. She was going to give him his usual Tab, but after what Violet said, and knowing they only had a few more days to go, she thought she could afford to be sadistic. She sang happily to herself as she carried the tray to his bedroom.

When she opened the door, she found him sitting in bed, reading a magazine. She went in and set the tray down. "Good news today," she told him. "I think we'll be wrapping up this project by the end of the week."

"It might even be sooner that that," he said, smugly.

What the hell did he mean by that? He looked up and smiled as he stuck a french fry into his mouth. Then she shook her head and continued down the stairs. Nope. Nothing was wrong. He was simply getting used to it . . . and she had to remember he was nuts to begin with.

Violet marked off Thursday.

She and Judy sat in Hart's kitchen. The week had gone by without a hitch. Hart was behaving himself. Violet smiled at Judy. "Tomorrow's the big day. The invoices will be here at nine o'clock on the button."

"We did it." Judy rested her head on her elbow. "We really did it."

"I'm going home," Violet said, getting up. "I'll see you at the office, and the minute work is through, the three of us will march in here and show him the goods we got on him. We get his promise, he gets ours, and that's that. But first, I'm gonna make sure I stick a copy of the invoices into my safe-deposit box."

"Absolutely."

Violet grabbed her car keys. "Till tomorrow, and the end of all this."

"Good night."

The sun was just barely rising when the phone began to jingle in the Rhodes house. Dwayne pulled the covers over his head. Doralee reached out and answered it. Her heart was in her throat.

"Hello?"

"Doralee?" the woman said.

Doralee felt her heart beating again. Thank God, it wasn't Judy. Or Violet.

"Who's calling?"

"Missy Hart."

"Oh, Mrs. Hart, hello."

"I hope I didn't wake you. Frank told me not to call anybody at the office, but I guess it's okay to call you at home. I wanted to thank you."

"Thank me?"

"Yes. I just realized it must have been you who sent me those bouquets of lovely flowers during my trip. You signed Frank's name."

"Well . . . it was his idea." Then Doralee realized the woman had said "during." What did she mean by that?

"No, it wasn't his idea at all," Missy Hart squeaked. "I asked him point-blank. You see, that's why I came back early, because I was touched by his thoughtfulness. It's so unlike him."

Doralee's voice turned to ice. Stunned, she could barely get out the words. "What? Did you say you've *come back* early?"

"Yes."

God Almighty! "Missy, listen to me, don't go home! Don't go home, not just yet. Um . . . come here." Doralee's head felt as though it was going to burst. "No, no, go to a hotel. Yes, a hotel. There's a big surprise—I can't tell you anything about it—till Saturday—yes, that's it, Saturday, you can go home on Saturday. . . ."

Missy was laughing. "Doralee, I'm *at* a hotel. I've been out jogging around the grounds for an hour already. I got home three days ago."

"Three days ago?"

"Yes. Frank sent me to the hotel for a week. He's doing some kind of exercise program at the house. My goodness, you should see what he's done to our bedroom, well, it's just—"

Doralee smashed her fist into the cradle of the phone. She took a deep breath. Then she lifted her hand and shakily dialed a number she knew well.

Violet was in her dressing gown, making herself an early morning cup of tea. The phone rang and she reached for it before it had a chance to wake the kids up. "Hello."

"Violet, this is Doralee. The job's up."

"What?"

"Missy Hart just called me. She's been home for three whole days."

"That's impossible."

"It's true!"

"But she hasn't been home because—"

"Are you sitting down?" Doralee asked.

"No."

"Do it."

Violet sat. "Okay. What?"

"Hart sent her to a hotel. Told her he was doing some new exercise program—she even told me what he did to the lousy bedroom."

"Doralee," Violet moaned.

"I know, I know. If she's been there and seen it and he sent her outta there, he must have been free for the last three days. Violet, what do we do? What kind of a game has he been playing on *us?*"

"The smarmy bastard," Violet hissed. "We've been *had.*"

"Don't be silly," Judy said. "I just brought him his breakfast. He's tied up like always."

"Or he's *pretending* to be tied up," Doralee said tensely.

"It can't be." Judy put her juice down and pulled the muffin from the toaster.

"Look, I'm coming over. Keep a hold of my gun and just sit tight until I get there." Doralee hung up.

Judy hung up.

And Hart hung up. He'd been listening on the extension in the upstairs hall. He backed into the shadows and waited.

Judy thought about it. Doralee was crazy. It *couldn't* be true. Why would he have *pretended* to be tied up for three whole days? Why submit to that torture? He'd have flown the coop as fast as—

But a creepy feeling came over her as she dressed for work. She knew she'd better check him one more time, just to play safe. But with Doralee's gun in her hand this time. She went to the drawer where she kept it. The drawer was empty. Maybe it was in the chest of drawers upstairs.

Judy hurried up the stairs. But she didn't get to the landing. She stopped in midair. The gun she was looking for had found her. Hart stood at the top of the stairs, pointing it directly at her astonished face.

Violet asked herself the same question that had gone through Judy's mind. Why would he have pretended to be tied up for three whole days? She knew there was only one possible answer, and if she was correct, she'd have to admit he was a *clever* bastard.

She gunned the engine and drove out to the Ajax Warehouse. She made her way over the debris and hoisted herself up onto an empty oil drum and looked through a broken window.

Her face fell. Ajax Warehouse was crammed with shipping crates and packing cases of all sizes.

Violet ran back to her car and took off in a cloud of dust.

Doralee screeched to a stop at Hart's front door, the right wheels of the car up on the bricks surrounding the flower bed. She hurried in and dashed up the stairs.

Rounding the corner to the landing, she ran into Judy. "Oh, God," Doralee cried, "tell me I was wrong, tell me—"

Judy gave her a dejected shrug and pointed to the bottom of the stairs.

"Oh, no." Doralee looked down. There was Hart, gun in hand, snickering to himself as he kicked the front door closed. "Well," she yelled at him, "you've got some nerve!"

"I'm sorry, Doralee," Judy said, sadly. "He found your gun."

"Well, girls," Hart cackled, "how's it feel to have the tables turned?"

"Up yours," Doralee snapped. She asked Judy, "You okay?"

"Yes. But I think we're in big trouble."

"You sure as shootin' are," Hart said, waving them down. "Come on, we're going for a ride."

Judy suddenly had terror in her eyes. "God knows what he's capable of now, he's so deranged after being in there for six weeks."

"What are you two whispering about?" Hart called.

Doralee ignored him. "We don't have a choice it seems, we gotta go with him. But what about Violet?"

"He doesn't seem to care."

Hart opened the front door. "Come on, come on."

"You think we should stall for her?" Doralee asked.

"I think we have a better chance if we go with him. At least Violet can *do* something, she won't have a gun pointed at her."

"Cut the whispering and get your butts down here!" Hart shouted.

"You don't have to scream," Doralee said, taking Judy's hand, walking down the stairs.

He motioned them out the front door. "Into the car."

"What car?" Doralee asked.

"This car."

She held out the keys.

He was incensed. *"I'm* not driving, you idiot— *you* are."

She went around and got in, muttering, "Never heard of the prisoner driving . . ."

"You," he said to Judy, "in the middle."

"I'm used to it." She got in.

He slid in next to her. He put one arm over the back of the seat and held the gun pointed at Judy with his other hand. "Okay, get this heap off my flowers and onto the street. And don't try anything funny or she gets it. Understand?"

Doralee started the car. "Got it."

They pulled away.

Violet pulled up. She had missed them by less than a minute.

She flung open the bedroom door. Hart's empty harness dangled from the ceiling. "Damn!" she cried, turning around, hurrying back to her car. She threw it into gear, and driving right over the grass, she hit the road with a squeal.

Doralee piloted the car into the Consoidated Building. She rolled down her window and shoved her card into the slot. The gate went up and she eased through, turning down to the basement's lower-level garage.

"No, no," Hart cursed, "not down there. *This* floor."

"This is the executive floor," she barked. "I can't park here."

"*I'm* an executive and I'm not going to humiliate myself any further by having to wait for a regular elevator down in that pit."

"Suit yourself." Doralee swung the wheel and the car careened around the bend, nicking Chuck Strell's Mercedes.

"Be careful!" Hart yelled.

"Stop shouting!" Doralee shouted back. "How do you expect a person to drive when you keep shouting? You make me nervous."

"I make *you* nervous? That's pretty funny coming from someone who tried to kill me. That's my space over there."

"I know, I know, I take your car to be washed every Tuesday, remember?"

They parked and got out.

"Now, the gun's in my pocket," Hart said. "You two stay ahead of me and don't try anything funny."

"We're not feeling particularly humorous today," Judy said.

Hart pushed the button for the executive elevator.

"Just what are your plans for us, Lieutenant Kojak?" Doralee asked.

"Never mind. You'll find out soon enough—when the ringleader of the group shows up."

"We're in this together," Doralee said. "You can't blame Violet any more than us."

The doors opened. "Okay, musketeers, inside." Then he got in, pushed *16,* and the doors shut. The elevator stopped on the twelfth floor.

Eddie Smith stepped on, wearing a snappy suit and tie. "Hey, girls," he said, "what's happening? Oh, Mr. Hart, good to see you."

Hart looked shocked.

"I want to shake your hand." Eddie held his out.

"Who are you?" Hart asked.

"Eddie Smith. Used to be in the mail room, but I took advantage of that new job rotation plan of yours and moved over to personnel. I'm having a ball."

"Huh?" Hart said.

"You're something else, Mr. Hart!" Eddie still held out his hand.

Finally, Hart pulled his right hand out of his pocket and accepted Eddie's. "Nice to meet you." Then he shoved it back in to grab the gun.

Eddie smiled from ear to ear, watching the *15* light up. "Just wanted to thank you, man." The doors opened. "Things are really jumping around here, huh, Judy?"

"Sure are," Judy said, looking at an unsmiling Hart.

"Remember when I felt this place was a prison?" Eddie asked, holding his hand on the door to prevent it from shutting. "Don't you believe it."

"That's easy for you to say," Judy answered. "You don't have a gun pointed at your back."

Hart stiffened.

Eddie laughed and waved.

The doors closed again.

"I didn't like that crack," Hart snapped.

"What are you so uptight about?" Judy snapped right back. "You've got us. We admit it. You don't have to be such a bully."

"After what you did to me, calling me a bully?"

"Oh, stop yelling," Doralee put in.

"You keep your trap shut. What was that stuff about job rotation?"

"Uh—" Judy didn't know what to say.

Doralee did. "While you were away, we managed to make a few changes."

His eyebrows stood up. "Changes? What kind of changes?"

The elevator doors opened and he saw for himself. "Holy shit," he gasped.

"Told you he wouldn't like it," Doralee mumbled.

Hart stared in amazement. Desks were rearranged, regrouped, with new dividers and—God, could it be—sofas? Yes, sofas, arranged in a little kind of parlor in the middle of the floor. And on a table in the setting was a coffee machine—a coffee machine right there in the office.

He looked to his right. There was a huge plant on a desk, so bushy he couldn't see who was working there. "What the hell is that?"

"Jennie Anderson. She loves gardening," Judy explained. "Her output has increased fifteen percent because of the new environment."

"Environment, horse shit." He looked to his left. A young man was sitting on a desk where another young man was having a cup of coffee. "What's going on there? Who's that person?"

"Which one?" Judy asked.

"The one sprawled on the desk. How dare he! He's fired."

"You can't fire him," Doralee explained. "He doesn't work here."

Hart was incensed. "Doesn't work here? Then what in the hell is he doing here?"

"Visiting his friend. You allow visitors on breaks, if they don't get in the way." Doralee smiled at the worker at the desk. "Hi, Patrick," she waved.

"How dare you?" Hart hissed. "Look. He's not even wearing a tie."

"Men don't have to any longer," Judy said. "Your new rules allow just about any kind of dress code that's comfortable."

"*My* new rules?" He faced Doralee again. "And what did you say, *I* allow visitors?"

"That's right," Doralee said.

"Then the one *behind* the desk is fired. And you can tell his boyfriend to get his ass off that desk, they can both clear on out."

"I'm afraid you can't do that, not unless you want Mr. Hinkle to jump down your back," Judy explained.

"Hinkle? What's Hinkle got to do with him?"

"Patrick's done such a fine job, he's being promoted, up to Hinkle's floor. Hinkle himself asked for the most qualified, and you suggested Patrick."

Hart did a slow burn. "Jesus Christ Almighty. *How* did all this happen? How did *I* authorize all this idiocy?"

Doralee pointed to the bulletin board. Hart read a memo announcing an office party the following week, proceeds to be donated toward getting an office TV set, so workers could watch the soaps during breaks or lunch hours. "It was one of my suggestions," Judy said, "that you approved wholeheartedly."

"See," Doralee pointed, "it's your signature."

Hart scrutinized it. Sure was. He cursed the day he taught Doralee to sign his checks. "Very funny." Then, suddenly, something occurred to him—it wasn't nine o'clock yet. "What are all these people doing here, working at this hour?"

"Well, you started another program called 'Flexible Hours.' People can set their own time. Patrick is on break now, which means he's been here since six. Some work eight to four, some ten to six, some nine to five, and a few, like Pat, come real early. It's a sensational success, because the building is always open anyhow,

and the cleaning people are done for the day by three
in the morning."

"It will be great in the summer," Doralee said,
"when everyone will want to go to the beach around
one or so."

"The beach!" he sputtered. "Well, I'm going to
put a stop to all this right away. Walk."

"Pardon me?" Doralee said.

"I still have a gun pointed at you."

"I forgot."

"Walk!"

"You don't have to shout!" Doralee turned and
started down the aisle, which now was carpeted.

Judy followed with Hart right behind her. She
motioned to the desks. "It's working nicely, Mr. Hart.
Everyone is more diligent and enthused in their new
creative atmosphere. Everyone's much more comfortable."

"Shut up and walk."

"A lot less absenteeism," Doralee chimed in.
"People like it a lot."

"Do they?" Hart snapped, having to smile at
some worker who was smiling at him as if he were
God. "Yippee. But I *hate* it, and what I say,
goes."

"Sure does," Judy mumbled.

"Keep walking and button that trap. Right to my
office. We'll wait in there till I'm ready to call the
cops." He looked around him as he followed them.
Someone had a photo of a cat on their desk. Another
woman had a blow-up of a semi-nude muscle man.
"This is disgusting. I've got to talk to Roz."

"Fat chance," Doralee cracked.

"Stop."

Doralee and Judy stopped walking.

"Why can't I talk to her?" He looked pale.

"Because she went on a little trip," Doralee said,
smiling.

Hart's face dropped. "Oh, no. Oh, my God, you
got Roz too? No . . . what did you do to her . . . you
couldn't have—"

"Now, don't cry," Doralee mocked, "she's just fine. She took a little trip to Aspen."

"Aspen?"

"Colorado," Judy interjected.

"I know where it is. What's she doing there? She doesn't ski. It isn't her vacation time."

"She's going to school," Doralee replied.

"Going to—" He shook his head. "You're both lunatics. I'll get on the phone to her as soon as we're in the office. *March.*"

Doralee began to walk toward his door again. "All I can say is, I hope you're up on your French."

Violet's blood ran cold when she saw Doralee's car in Hart's space. She crossed her fingers and hurried upstairs.

When the doors opened, a girl from the mail room rushed to Violet. "These came for you special delivery from the New York office, Miss Newstead."

Violet took the big manila envelope. "Fat lot of good it's gonna do me now." She ran through the main aisle and opened Hart's door.

"Violet, we've been expecting you." Hart glared at her from behind his desk.

Violet turned to Judy and Doralee on the sofa. "You okay?"

"Fine, fine," Doralee said, filing her nails, "just having a wonderful day."

"Here," Violet shouted, tossing the thick envelope into Hart's arms. "Those are the invoices we've been waiting for. But you've made them worthless." She turned to the girls again. "For the last three days, he's managed to put all the missing equipment and supplies back into the warehouse."

"So *that's* why he pretended!" Judy said.

Doralee stabbed the leather sofa with her nail file. "The nerve."

"It cost me a lot of money to set that right," Hart said with a smirk, and tossed the invoices into the trash can.

Violet folded her arms. "Well, you've won. You trumped our ace. So what are you going to do now?"

"Sit down, Violet," he said, calmly. "I'm gonna play the very last card. I'm gonna send you three bitches to jail."

Violet sat with Judy and Doralee.

Just then the phone rang; without thinking, Doralee answered it. "Mr. Hart's office, can I help—?" She stopped herself and looked at the other two. "What am I doing?" She slammed the phone back down.

"Don't do that!" Hart shouted, grabbing his receiver. "Hello? Hello?" He glared at Doralee. "Who was that?"

"I don't know. I think it was Hinkle himself. But who cares? I don't work here anymore."

"Hinkle!" Hart dialed the phone as fast as he could. "Gotta get things back the way they were before he hears what's going on down—" He cleared his throat. "Hello, yes, is Mr. Hinkle in? Yes, this is Frank Hart. Um, he just tried to call me and we got cut off. Yes, thanks." He narrowed his eyes at Doralee. "You'll do *double* time, you little—" He snapped to attention. His voice changed. "Oh, yes, Mr. Hinkle, no, I don't know what happened, we got disconnected somehow—now, come on, would we hang up on the president of the company?"

Doralee mimicked putting her finger down her throat.

"What? He's *here?* In town? In the *building!* Oh, dear God—it can't be true—holy shit." He jumped up. "No, no problem at all. Thanks." He hung up and hurried around the desk. He looked stricken.

"What's the matter with you?" Doralee asked. "Somebody put rat poison in your ear?"

"Worse. Tinsworthy's here."

"Who?" Judy asked.

"Tinsworthy," Hart repeated.

Violet covered her mouth. "Oh, boy."

"Who's Tinsworthy?" Judy asked.

"Tinsworthy!" Hart screamed at her. "The chairman of the board!"

"I don't even know what this damn company does, much less I should know the name of the chairman of the board," Judy muttered.

Hart was trembling. "Russel Tinsworthy, the goddamn chairman of the board, and he's on his way down here to meet me." Hart pressed his knees together, shaking. "Violet, you've got to help me. You've got to stick by me. I'll ... I'll give you leniancy, a reduced sentence. I promise, we'll blame it all on them. Come on." He opened the door and rushed out.

Violet gave the other two a nod and got up with a smile. They followed Hart into the big office.

"Holy shit," Hart muttered, holding on to Doralee's desk. "He's here already."

The man was easy to find. Distinguished-looking, silver-haired, and in his eighties, Russel Tinsworthy had the bearing and personal authority of a retired army general as he stood chatting with some of the workers. He towered over everyone. He shook hands with Maria Delgrado and slapped Tom Wood on the shoulders And he was smiling as he came directly toward Hart with a bottle of champagne in his hand. Behind him was President Hinkle and a thin man with an odd face whom Violet realized she'd seen around the office in the past weeks.

"Here's the man himself, Mr. Tinsworthy," Hinkle said as they came within speaking distance. "This is Franklin Hart."

Tinsworthy extended his hand and gripped Hart's limp arm with a strong handshake. He held out the champagne. With a low, aristocratic voice, he said, "Hart, a token of my esteem."

Bewildered, Hart accepted the bottle, and exchanged glances with Violet. "Th ... thank you, Mr. Tinsworthy. It's certainly nice to see you."

"Well, I don't spend a lot of time out here," Tinsworthy said, an arm over Hart's shoulder, "but Perkins here"—the thin man nodded to the group—"he keeps me informed, keeps tabs on what's going on.

And when a division shows a twenty percent rise in productivity in only six weeks time, I personally want to meet the man responsible."

Doralee thought she was going to faint.

Judy gasped.

Violet smirked as only Violet could do.

"Thank you," Hart said, brightening up. "Yes, thank you. I appreciate that." Violet coughed. "I mean *we* appreciate that," he corrected.

"Don't be modest," Tinsworthy said, looking around, beaming. "What an excellent environment you've created around here. Very livable. Very personal." A woman carried a baby through the center of the data processing section.

Hart thought he was going to die.

Tinsworthy nodded to the woman, approvingly. "Yes siree, Hart. Can I call you Frank?"

Tinsworthy turned to the president. "You know, Hinkle, I'd like to see this kind of arrangement implemented throughout all of Consolidated. It's a great credit to Frank, here."

Hart sounded more sure of himself now. "Yes, it's very . . ." The thought of it still made him sick. But he had to say *something*. "Well, the people like it."

"Keep the crew happy, Frank," Tinsworthy spouted, "and the ship won't go down. Can't go wrong if you please the workers."

Hinkle said, "Mr. Tinsworthy is interested in some of the new programs of yours."

"Yes," Tinsworthy said, "like that job sharing idea. A bold move."

Judy beamed.

"Job sharing?" Hart asked. "Or do you mean job posting?"

"Both. How're they working out?"

"Um, Violet . . ." She took a step forward. "Mr. Tinsworthy, this is Violet Newstead, my senior supervisor."

She shook the chairman's hand. "I'm very happy to meet you, Mr. Tinsworthy."

"Likewise. I've heard some wonderful reports about you."

Violet blushed.

"She's my right hand around here," Hart said, pompously. Doralee held her throat. "Violet," Hart offered, "tell Mr. Tinsworthy about our job sharing situation."

Violet did, gladly. "It's proved very effective so far. Maria Delgrado over there—I believe you've met her—she's a good example. She shares that job with another worker who takes over in the afternoon."

"She does?" Hart said. Then he corrected himself. "I mean, she does."

"Both women are happy," Violet explained, "and we've been more than pleased with their performance."

Tinsworthy made a fist and playfully socked Hart in the shoulder. "You pulled it off!"

"We like to think so, sir," Hart replied.

"Like the Day Care Center."

"What did you say, Mr. Tinsworthy?" Hart asked.

Tinsworthy sat on Doralee's desk. "You know, I had a hand in setting up day-care centers at all the defense plants during the war. Kept our women working on the assembly lines. Cost was minimal. Glad to see you've brought it back."

Hart was shocked. He felt like the guys he read about who stayed on jungle islands for years and years after the war was over, thinking it was still on, and then came back into the world in total shock. "Yes, well . . ." What the hell to say? He didn't even know where the Day Care Center *was*. "Violet?"

"Come," Violet said, "it's just down the hall."

"Thank you, my dear," Tinsworthy replied, extending his arm for Violet. "I can see why Frank has such *trust* in you."

Violet shot Hart a look he'd never forget. "Well," she said, "things have been a little *up in the air* in his personal life lately, so I try to do my best here so he won't have to worry about too much." Then Violet led Tinsworthy, Hinkle and Perkins down the hall.

Hart handed Doralee the bottle of champagne. "Now, listen to me, I don't want to hear a crack out of either of you," he warned. "You *owe* me one. Now, where the hell is this kiddie's playroom?"

"Remember the old storage room?" Judy answered.

"Good place for 'em," Hart said.

"You should see it now," Doralee replied.

Suddenly, Margaret Foster came down the aisle and stopped Hart as he started toward the storage room. She was dressed in designer jeans and a fluffy print blouse, and her hair had been restyled. The newest feature was her eyes—they sparkled right along with her personality. She looked fifteen years younger. "Mr. Hart, it's so good to see you again."

"Who are *you?*"

"Don't you recognize me? Margaret Foster."

Hart was baffled. "You're that old lush."

"Yes, that was me, but thanks to the company's alcoholic rehabilitation program, those days are over."

He was baffled. "Alcoholic rehab—"

"You started it," Judy muttered.

"Oh, right." He beamed.

"I'm so grateful to Consolidated for paying for my weeks at the clinic," Margaret said, "and I'll never forget you and those wonderful notes of encouragement you sent. It is touching when management cares so much." She kissed him on the cheek. "God bless you, Mr. Hart."

"Your new program for Working Expectant Mothers is a hit as well," Doralee said.

He was in pain. "Later," he said, hurrying down the hall to the storage room.

Judy and Doralee tagged along.

"Holy shit again," he said, walking in the door. The crummy dungeon was transformed into a bright, spacious kindergarten filled with tots. There were all kinds of toys and plastic furniture, a blackboard for lessons, even a piano that had been painted yellow, like the walls.

Tinsworthy was playing with a rocking horse.

"I've got to hand it to you, my boy," he said, looking up at Hart. "You've really pulled it off. I love children, don't you?"

Hart forced a smile.

"Oh, he does, Mr. Tinsworthy," Violet said. "In fact, I've heard he turned part of his house into a kind of *jungle-gym.*"

"Hart, you're my man," Tinsworthy said, pulling Hart out of the room. In the hall, he whispered, "Of course, that equal pay business will have to go. It was a good incentive, but there's no need to keep priming the pump."

"Damn," Judy whispered.

"It's only *one* strikeout," Doralee reminded her.

"You're my kind of guy, Frank," Tinsworthy continued. "Creative, incisive, get-the-job-done. I've been talking to Hinkle. I want you to come work with me."

Hart froze. "Excuse me?"

"A voice from heaven," Violet said to Judy and Doralee.

"I need a man like you, Frank," Tinsworthy explained.

"Please, God," Violet prayed, "to the moon, send him to the moon."

Tinsworthy continued, "The Brazilian operation is just beginning to take off."

"Brazil?" Hart sounded feeble.

Violet said, "Well, not the moon, maybe, but far enough, right?"

"You'll love it down there, Frank," the old man bellowed. "Healthy climate—you could use a little color." He patted Hart's cheek. "You've been spending too much time indoors."

Doralee choked.

At the executive elevator, Hart made his plea. "But, sir, Mr. Chairman, I can't move to Brazil."

"You'll get a healthy bonus and you'll be doing a big favor to me and the company. Besides, Perkins tells me your wife likes to travel."

"But my job here . . . the responsibilities—"

"You've set them on the right course," Tinsworthy said. "It's time for a new challenge. Let your subordinates take over. You told me you trust Violet here."

Violet beamed.

"Right, Hinkle?" Tinsworthy asked.

"Anything you say, R.T."

The elevator doors opened. "Come on up to my office, Frank," Tinsworthy said, "and we'll work things out. I want you on my team right away."

Hart was trembling. "Sir, I appreciate your confidence in me, but—"

"Teamwork!" Tinsworthy got into the elevator as if boarding an airplane that was going to bomb the enemy. "Teamwork, Hart! Go where you're most needed."

"But Mr. Tinsworthy . . ."

"Frank," old R.T. said in a tone he hadn't used before, "I'll tell you right now, I'm not the kind of man who takes *no* for an answer."

Hart looked resignedly at Violet, Doralee, and Judy. "Brazil?" he said, "I guess it could be worse."

Doralee uncorked the bottle and foam splashed all over Hart's desk. She filled three coffee mugs with the bubbly liquid.

"To F. Hart," Violet toasted.

"And to old R.T.," Doralee added.

"And the jungles of Brazil!" Judy sang, clinking her mug against theirs.

Judy closed her eyes and grinned. "Oh, did you see the look on his face?"

Violet nodded and put her feet up on his desk, trying out his chair for size. "So help me, I almost felt sorry for him. Remember I said *almost*."

Judy set her mug down and leaned forward, resting her chin on her hands, elbows on the desk. "We did it," she said, happily. "We pulled it off. We didn't panic."

"We did more than we ever dreamed we were going to do," Doralee said with pride. "And Tinsworthy loved it."

"Except for the money part," Judy reminded her.

"Don't worry," Violet said, "we'll get that back into effect in no time. This is only the beginning."

"I'll drink to that!" Doralee sang

"I'll drink to this company," Judy said. "You know, it's really not a bad place at all . . . even if nobody knows what we actually make."

"I think it's nuts and bolts," Violet said, and she started laughing.

"I'll drink to that!" Doralee said, and they lifted their glasses again.

And then there was a knock on the door. *"Monsieur Hart!"*

"Oh, no," Violet squealed, leaning back in Hart's chair, "I forgot all about her."

Another knock. *"C'est moi!"*

Doralee called out, "Come in, honey," and stretched out across the top of the desk, the champagne bottle in her hand.

The door opened and Roz walked in, wearing a beret pulled down over her bun, smiling brightly.

"Hi, Roz," Violet said.

Roz dropped her purse. "Holy Merde!" she replied.

ABOUT THE AUTHOR

THOM RACINA is the author of over ninety books (under almost as many names). He put himself through the Art Institute of Chicago by writing paperback novels during the week and children's plays on the weekends. Mr. Racina has also written two musicals, *Allison Wonderland* and *Marvelous Misadventures of Sherlock Holmes*, for which he penned the book, music and lyrics. He has written novels based on the TV series "Quincy," "Baretta," and "Kojak" and has written several books based on film scripts, among them *Lifeguard* and *FM*. A contributing editor to such magazines as *Cosmopolitan*, *Playboy* and *Penthouse*, Mr. Racina is currently at work on both a novel and a screenplay.

Bantam Book Catalog

Here's your up-to-the-minute listing of over 1,400 titles by your favorite authors.

This illustrated, large format catalog gives a description of each title. For your convenience, it is divided into categories in fiction and non-fiction—gothics, science fiction, westerns, mysteries, cookbooks, mysticism and occult, biographies, history, family living, health, psychology, art.

So don't delay—take advantage of this special opportunity to increase your reading pleasure.

Just send us your name and address and 50¢ (to help defray postage and handling costs).